And Tell Tchaikovsky the News

Robert Lamb

Red Letter Press

Columbia Atlanta Charleston

Est. 1998

For all my sons

In Memoriam

Paul Douglas Hale (1940-2014)

Chapter One

Time: The Not-Too-Distant Future

BILLY PAID little attention when he saw the old man pull up to the garage one fine spring morning and begin unloading the truck. Nothing about the man's appearance was unusual. He was black and muscular, with hair beginning to gray, and the truck was showing its age, too. It soon became evident that the man was moving into the apartment over the garage, but handymen came and went. Billy's father was always complaining about the unreliability of

3

hired help, both at home and at his radio stations. Billy went back to his violin practice.

But a few minutes later, he was drawn to his window again. The old man was still trudging up and down the stairs, hauling boxes, and lugging suitcases and a few clothes on hangers, but apparently he had already rigged up his stereo and turned it on. Music flowed out the open windows of the garage apartment, drifted across the pool and courtyard, and wafted through the open windows of Billy's bedroom. Billy listened. The music was unfamiliar, but he liked what he heard. It had drive and verve, and the beat seemed to run straight from his ears to his feet. He looked at his violin and put it aside. Then he moved back to the window, cranked it open wider, and sat on the window seat to listen. Now a man was singing in a clear, impassioned voice that seemed to bounce along for a while on top of a strong bass line and then slide into a squeal of – what exactly? Mock anger? Comic frustration?

Whatever it was, it was certainly rhythmic. And strangely happy. Whether truly upset or simply play-acting, the singer obviously was having a very good time even if singing about a bad time. Billy listened more closely, the toes of one tennis-shod foot tapping on the floor, the long fingers of one hand tapping on the window sill.

". . .bought you a brand new Mustang, a nineteen sixty-five; now you come around signifying, woman, you don't wanna let me ride. Mustaaaang Sally, now, baby…"

The music was rock 'n' roll – Billy knew that much – but he didn't recognize the tunes – not the one playing now or any of the others that followed. His parents' taste in music ran to classical, he himself was schooled in band and chamber music – the violin practice was for the octet in which he played – and the radios in the

5

house stayed tuned to WSOF, his father's soft-music station in Atlanta.

"All that other stuff is so much air pollution," Mr. Randolph was fond of saying. "Rap? It's fine – if you happen to be a Ubangi. Country? Music for mental retards. Hard rock? A nervous breakdown set to music." On and on and on he went. "New Wave? Mental masturbation for space cadets. Oldies? Look at the demographics: your audience is either dying or going deaf from old age. You're losing market share with every record you spin, with every day's newspaper obituaries. No, sir. Soft and soothing – that's the way to go. We may not *lead* the parade, but the parade won't leave us behind, either."

When his father got going like that, which it seemed was at least three times a week, usually at the supper table, Billy listened politely and said nothing. His mother invariably reminded his father that radio stations didn't "spin records" anymore, that everything was on tape, and encouraged him to "avoid using obsolete slang – it makes you sound unprofessional," but Mr. Randolph paid no attention. Or seemed not to. Billy had his doubts about his father's ideas, but what did a fifteen-year-old know about business? Still he couldn't help wondering if his father were wrong. Not about format. Billy didn't listen much to radio and didn't understand those who did, especially those – some of them his friends – who went around wearing earphones half the time. It was much more fun to hack away at his computer. But WSOF had been drifting lower in the ratings ever since he could remember. Eighteenth in a market of sixty. Was that okay? It didn't *sound* so hot. He could remember when the station was Number 3. In a market as big as Atlanta's, Number 3 sounded pretty good. Not terrific, but solid, respectable. But eighteenth? At best, it sounded so-so, and when you took into account that eighteenth for WSOF meant a slip of fifteen notches in three years, it sounded a lot worse. How far back in a parade could you fall before falling out of it altogether?

But that was no concern of his, he figured. Besides, his mind was on the music the old black man was playing. Now it had shifted almost imperceptibly from rock 'n' roll to something more complex, something similar but with a slower beat, and it featured the guitar instead of the saxophone. And what a guitar! Billy had never heard one like it – and he himself played guitar, played well, in fact. All his friends said so. But he didn't play like that! This guitar had a full, rich, authoritative sound that wailed up and down the scales, sometimes in a strutting bass, other times in cascading melodies, but all the time in a billowing of chords that rolled over the courtyard and into the morning air like joy set to music.

Unable to resist, Billy leaned out the window and spied the old man lifting a large box out of the back of his truck. "Hey, Mister," he called.

The man stopped and looked up and around until he saw Billy. "Hey," he called out. "Good morning."

"What's that music you're playing?" Billy said.

"Oh, so you like the blues, do you? That's Stevie Ray Vaughan on the guitar and vocal, 'You Better Leave My Little Girl Alone.' Sucker can sho nuff play, cain't he?" Under his breath, he added, "'Specially for a white boy." The man carried the box a few steps toward the garage apartment. Stopping for a breather at the foot of the stairs, he called to Billy again. "You live here?"

"Yes."

"I'm your new maintenance man, John Henry Jones."

"I'm Billy. Billy Randolph."

"Pleased to meet you," John Henry said, starting up the stairs. "Say, why ain't you in school?"

"School's out. Last Friday was the last day. Need help with that?"

John Henry stopped and put down the box. "Don't mind if I do."

"Be right down."

A minute later, Billy Randolph burst out the back door of the house, nearly taking the screen door off its hinges. On the run, he crossed the forty yards between the house and the garage in seconds. "Let me help with that, Mr. Jones." He pointed to the box beside John Henry.

"Just John Henry." He stuck out his hand for Billy to shake. "You don't call me *Mister* Jones and I won't call you Mr. Randolph."

Billy laughed and shook hands on it. Peering into the box, which was filled to overflowing with phonograph records, he said, "What're those?"

"They're called records. They don't make 'em anymore. CD's replaced them." "Oh. Is that where the music's coming from?"

"Yeah. You must like music."

"I do."

"Rock 'n' roll." It was a statement, not a question.

"Never heard much of it till now."

John Henry did a double take. "Where you been?"

"Right here," Billy said, waving an arm to indicate the immediate environs, but meaning Atlanta.

"You a prisoner here?" John Henry smiled and jerked his head toward the big house. "Cut off from civilization or something?"

Billy laughed. "No! What made you think that?"

"How old are you?"

"Sixteen. Well, soon, anyhow."

John Henry shook his head. "I never before met a boy your age who didn't know rock 'n' roll."

Billy's smile faded. "My father's in radio," he explained. "Station WSOF, soft music around the clock. In our house, we can either listen to WSOF or find something else to do." He brightened. "I'm in the school band, though. And I belong to a chamber music group."

"Classical?"

"Yep," Billy said. "Violin. Guitar, too, on some numbers we do. English airs, mostly." He frowned.

John Henry pointed to the box of records. "No classical music in there. No English airs, either. Sorry."

"What *is* in there?"

"Oh, a little Ray Charles, for instance. Know him?"

Billy shook his head no.

"Hmm. How 'bout the Godfather of Soul, James Brown? Or the Shirelles?"

No.

"Aretha Franklin? Gladys Knight? B. B. King? Otis Redding? The Supremes?"

No.

"This is serious, man. Wilson Pickett? Mary Wells, Ben E. King?" He broke into song as if to spur Billy's memory: "*There is a rose in Spanish Harlem. . .*" No? How 'bout Marvin Gaye?"

No, no, no, no.

John Henry beamed. "I got you now! The Beatles."

No.

"Elvis!"

No.

"This is way past serious. You know that, don't you?"

Billy looked as if he had just learned that he flunked an algebra test.

John Henry put a consoling hand on his shoulder. "Hear that?" he asked. From the stereo in the apartment overhead came the strains of "Stubborn Kind of Fellow." The infectious rhythm had reached Billy's brain before it reached his consciousness, and he was already tapping a foot to the tune: "...*but every time I reach for you, Baby, you just jump clean out of sight. . . Guess I'm just a stubborn kinda fellow, got my mind made up to love you.*"

"Now, Brother, that cat could sing," John Henry said. "Marvin Gaye."

"Could? Did something happen to him?"

"Dead now. Shot by his own father. Tragic." John Henry flashed a big smile. "But it's also tragic that a young fellow like you don't know who he was."

"Sorry."

"Don't look so sad. Fortunately for you, Billy boy, all the material for Remedial Rock 'n' Roll is right here in this box." He stabbed at the box with a toe. "Not to mention a few more boxes I already hauled in. Reckon your daddy will let you listen?"

"He's never said not to. Just not on the radios in the house. Besides, lately he's hardly ever around."

"Well, I wouldn't want to go against his word. That wouldn't be right. Besides, I need the job. So if he tells you not to do it, be sure to let me know."

Billy smiled. "Okay." He paused. "Then there's Mr. Montrose, my music teacher. He hates *everything* modern." Billy smiled. "But he's not around much either. His real job, general manager of Dad's radio station, keeps him pretty busy." He leaned down to pick up the box and was surprised to find it so heavy.

15

His face turned red from the strain and he stood up puffing.

"Here," said John Henry. "Let's tackle this together. A job like this calls for teamwork."

In the next hour, John Henry put away his clothes and arranged his personal belongings while Billy organized his records, dusting them and stacking them on end in alphabetical order by artist. He relished the job: he could read the covers on the albums while listening to the music. And on and on the music went, with somebody named Lee Dorsey *"working in a coal mine,"* a woman named Mary Wells beating somebody to the punch, and a frenetic voice belonging to somebody named James Brown who proclaimed in a funky rhythm punctuated by staccato brass, *"I feel good!"*

Billy felt good, too, and the more of that music he heard, the better he felt. But soon he heard a familiar voice coming from the back stoop of his house. "Uh, oh," he said, scrambling to his feet. "That's Henrietta, our housekeeper," he informed John Henry. "Got to go. I promised to unload the dishwasher."

"Come back anytime."

"Can I bring a friend next time?"

"Bring anybody you please. My house is yo' house." John Henry laughed at his own joke.

"My friend's got to hear this music of yours."

John Henry smiled. "He been livin' on another planet, too?"

Billy blushed. "No, but he's been in the hospital a lot. Something's wrong with one of his legs. Lame, I think. And he can't talk."

"Can't talk? Why not?"

Billy shrugged his shoulders. He didn't know.

John Henry smiled. "Don't matter. By all means, bring him."

Billy unloaded the dishwasher while Henrietta grilled him on the new yardman. On a kitchen counter nearby, soft music played on a portable radio tuned, as always, to WSOF.

"I see you met the new handy man." Billy was piling dishes on the counter and Henrietta was putting them up.

"Yeah."

"What did you think of 'im?"

"Nice."

"What's he like?"

"Nice."

"He got a name?"

"John Henry."

She smiled. Finally an answer of more than one word. "It was nice of you to help him move in."

"Yeah."

"How come you so talkative this morning?"

18

That snapped Billy out of the daze he was in, the kind in which youngsters simply tune out the adult world. Henrietta knew the phase well: kids know you're talking, but to them it sounds like adults in the "Peanuts" cartoons — "*wah, wah,*" like a horn blowing. She smiled, gave him a knowing look, and tousled his hair.

Embarrassed, Billy apologized for his inattention. "Sorry, Henrietta. I was thinking about John Henry's music."

"I heard some of it." She smiled. Then she scowled. "Yo' daddy better not hear it."

"Was it that loud?"

"Not really. Guess I was just listening hard."

"You liked it, too?"

"Oh, yeah. 'Specially my feet. 'Course, that's the music I grew up on."

"I can't wait till Dash hears it. When will he be back?" Dash was Henrietta's grandson, but he lived with her at the Randolphs'.

"This afternoon."

"Yes, but when?"

She looked at the clock on the kitchen wall. "His appointment was for 'leven. Speech therapy today." Under her breath she added "for all the good it'll do." Then she said, "He should be back by one, one-thirty."

It was eleven now. Billy started to leave the kitchen. He couldn't wait to get to his guitar so he could try out some of the chords and tunes still spinning around in his head, spinning like John Henry's records.

"You forgot the silverware."

"Oh." His shoulders slumped. He came back to the dishwasher and began handing the silverware to Henrietta, who wiped it dry and then put it away. He was nearly finished when his mother swept into the room, dressed to go out and in a hurry.

She gave Billy a perfunctory kiss, checked her appearance in a small mirror hanging on the inside of the pantry door, and asked both Henrietta and Billy, "How do I look?"

"Like you always look," Henrietta said. "Like you just stepped out of a band box."

Gloria Randolph smiled. "Thank you."

Billy didn't know what a band box was, but he knew that Henrietta had meant it as a compliment, and he agreed that his mother looked good. Very good. Gloria Randolph was a good-looking woman who knew how to dress, judging by all the other moms he knew. Tall and slender, she had green eyes and dark brown hair that was lustrous and full-bodied, and she always looked shower-fresh and neatly turned out.

A car horn sounded. "That's Peaches," she said. Moving hurriedly, she went toward the front door of the house, talking as she went and leaving a trail of wonderful fragrances that Billy followed for a few steps as if enchanted by them. "Got to run, Billy. Committee meeting at the club. Henrietta knows all about it. Don't forget to practice for the festival. Now be a good boy and mind Henrietta."

The club was the Piedmont Driving Club, one of Atlanta's oldest and most exclusive. The festival was the upcoming Piedmont Arts Festival, a big event held annually in the park and sponsored by the club in conjunction with the city. Billy's classical music octet would be performing there this year. *In fact, next month!* he remembered with a new and unfamiliar feeling of dread. His mind was no longer on classical music.

He went back into the kitchen, but only a moment later announced to Henrietta that he guessed he'd better "go practice for the festival." With that, he eased out of the room and raced off up the stairs.

He had meant it to sound properly dutiful, but he didn't fool Henrietta Powell for one minute. He and the group were ready for the festival anyhow. Had been practicing for weeks. And when moments later she heard Billy searching for the chords to Chuck Berry's *Memphis*, she smiled knowingly and began softly singing the words as he quickly found the right notes: *"Long distance information, give me Memphis, Tennessee. Help me find the party tryin' to get in touch with me. . ."*

In his apartment, John Henry heard it, too, and, smiling, went to his open door so he could hear better: *"She could not leave her number, but I know who placed the call, 'cause my uncle took the message and he wrote it on the wall."*

23

He grinned. *Not bad. Not bad, at all,* he thought. *Boy learns fast.* He went back inside to continue putting his new home in order.

Half an hour later, Billy knocked on the frame of his doorway. When John Henry looked around, pleasantly surprised, Billy said, "It's lunch time, and Henrietta said I could invite you to eat with me."

John Henry beamed. "Why, thanks, Billy. I'll be there soon as I wash up."

Chapter Two

"THIS KITCHEN is bigger than the whole house I grew up in," said John Henry. He was looking around the room in awe as he sipped iced tea after polishing off a tuna salad sandwich. Somewhere in the room, soft music played on a radio.

"Gosh," Billy said, his eyes sweeping the kitchen. Everybody he knew lived in a big house.

"Bigger than the house I grew up in, too," said Henrietta, who had eaten lunch with them and also was lingering over a glass of iced tea. They sat in the breakfast area, which occupied one spacious corner at one end of the big kitchen and overlooked the pool, the garage, and the grounds at the rear of the house.

"Where was that?" John Henry asked.

"Augusta."

"Augusta!" He grinned. "That's where I come from. Where in Augusta?"

"Turpin Hill, in a part of town called The Terri. I never knew why."

"Know it well," John Henry said, grinning. "I even know why they called it The Terri."

Henrietta gave him an inquisitive look.

"It was short for Negro Territory."

Henrietta laughed. "You don't say." Then they laughed together, and Henrietta asked, "What part of Augusta you from?"

"Grew up in a two-room shotgun house just a long nine-iron from the Augusta National Golf Club. Used to caddy there. It's where I learned grounds-keeping, too. It's also where I first saw how the other half lives." He looked around the bright, colorful kitchen again, shaking his head and saying, "Um, um." He gave Henrietta a look. "Some folks got it made, ain't they?"

"Yeah," she said. "Not all of them deserve it." She reached over and tousled Billy's hair. "But these folks do."

"Glad to hear it," John Henry said. "I sure am tired of working for those that don't."

"You'll like it here." She turned to Billy, sitting to her right. "Won't he, Billy?"

Billy grinned. "I sure hope so. I want to hear more of his records." He held up an empty mug. "Pass the milk, please."

Henrietta poured milk into Billy's mug while saying to John Henry, "Where you get all those old records?"

"In another life, I was a deejay," he said. "Some of the records were freebies from record companies. But I bought most of 'em with my own money, believe it or not." John Henry gave

27

a self-deprecating laugh "I've always spent money on music that I should have been spending on other things."

"Better than spending it on booze." Henrietta was sure of that. "Like my late husband."

"I spent some on booze, too," said John Henry, staring vacantly for a moment, as if looking inward at some melancholy aspect of his past. Then he gave Henrietta a level look. "But not anymore."

"Why you leave radio?"

"It was just a get-by job. I wanted to break into show biz."

"You a actor?" She pulled back to give him the once-over.

"*Noooo.*" He dragged out the vowel sound as if to emphasize how far off base her guess had been. "Dancer."

"What?"

"Dancer. Hoofer. Tap and soft shoe." With his fingers, he tapped out a snappy little rhythm on the table top. "Show biz. Song and dance man. Imitations." He stood up, broke into a Sammy Davis Jr. song, "Mr. Bojangles," and showed her a nimble step or two.

Henrietta's face lit up with joyous surprise. "Sound just like him!"

John Henry made a little bow. "Even played Vegas two or three times."

Henrietta laughed and clapped her hands. "Well, I declare! A singer *and* a dancer!" Suddenly she frowned. "What happened?"

John Henry reared back in exaggerated dismay. "What *didn't* happen? When's the last time you saw somebody tap dancing?"

"*Hmmm.*" Henrietta searched her memory. "Long time."

"Or soft-shoeing?"

"*Hmmm.*"

"My imitations never were *that* good," he said, shrugging, "and, anymore, tap dancing belongs to the Stone Age." He rolled his eyes and pulled a sad face. "Too, a man gets old, you know. Dancing's a young man's trade."

Henrietta made a clucking sound and fixed John Henry with an accusing stare. "You not that old."

"Fifty, come December the first. What about you?"

She considered lying, but finally said, "Fifty-two last month."

"*Naaa*," he said, waving a hand, looking her up and down. "No way."

With a toss of her head, she said, "Tell that to my bones." But she was pleased that he had not believed her, or at least had pretended so.

"How long you work for these folks?" John Henry asked.

"Long time. I come to work for the Randolphs right before this boy here was born." She tousled Billy's hair again. "I feel like he's as much mine as his mother's. He's fifteen."

"Fifteen and a half," Billy corrected.

"And you live here, too?" John Henry asked Henrietta.

"Sho' do. This is my home." She waved a hand to indicate the environs. "One of the guest houses behind the garage," she explained.

"Nice," he said. "No kinfolks?"

"Just my grandson, Dasher. Everybody call him Dash." She saw the puzzled look on John Henry's face. "His real name is 'Dashell,' But everybody call it 'Dasher' at first, then just 'Dash.' Don't ask me where his mother come up with the name 'Dashell.' I don't know, and never will. She's gone."

"Gone?" John Henry said.

"Passed over," she said after glancing cautiously at Billy. But then Billy excused

31

himself to go to his room. When he was out of earshot, Henrietta added: "Killed by a jealous wife in a nightclub brawl. Stabbed. She was a wild one, that girl. *My* girl, I mean."

"How old was your grandson when that happened?"

"Nine. Been with me ever since. He's fifteen now. "

"How'd he take it, his mother's death, I mean?" John Henry searched Henrietta's face with a look of concern.

Her eyes teared up. "Struck dumb and lame," she said. "Started walkin' again after a year. Still limps. But he ain't spoke a word since."

"Damn!" John Henry said softly and heaved a big sigh. Catching himself, he said, "Sorry. That just popped out."

She waved off his concern. "Many's the time I've felt damned." She got up to clear the table.

"You can say that again," said John Henry, getting up, too. "Here, let me help." He picked up his dishes.

She pointed. "Just put 'em in the sink. I'll get to 'em later."

At that moment, a young boy came into the kitchen through the back door. He stopped in his tracks when he saw John Henry.

"Dash!" Henrietta cried. She pointed to John Henry, who was standing by the kitchen sink. "This here's Mr. John Henry–" She stopped and looked at John Henry. "What *is* your last name?"

"Jones."

"This here's Mr. Jones. The new gardener," Henrietta said. "Mr. Jones, this is my grandson, Dash."

"Hi, Dash." John Henry smiled.

Staring at the floor, Dash made a sound that might have been intended as "hello," though maybe not.

"Hungry?" Henrietta asked him.

He shook his head to indicate no, eyes still focused on the floor.

"Miz Atkins bring you home?"

He nodded in the affirmative.

"She's the speech therapist," Henrietta explained to John Henry.

Just then, guitar music rolled down the stairs and spilled into the kitchen. Billy was practicing again. Dash looked at his grandmother expectantly.

She nodded toward the stairs. "Go ahead." She knew he wanted to join Billy. To John Henry, she said, "They in the school band together and some string outfit. Eight of 'em. A sextet? That the word?"

"Octet," John Henry said.

"Dash play bass in the band and octet, but piano be his first love. Play by ear, him and Billy both, but they take lessons, too, from ol' man Montrose."

34

John Henry watched the boy as he limped across the wide kitchen and into the hallway, listing slightly to one side, the right, on every other step. "What's wrong with his leg and vocal chords? Exactly, I mean?" John Henry asked.

"It ain't the leg *or* the vocal chords, if you ask me; it's the heart."

John Henry didn't say anything, but the expression on his face asked for an explanation.

"Leg looks whole. Vocal chords, too. X-rays don't show nothin' wrong. Doctors can't find nothin', either. But he ain't spoke or walked right since the day his mother got kilt." Henrietta looked sad and pointed to her temple. "Whatever's wrong is up here, I think – but I believe the hurt went in through the heart."

"*Um!*" John Henry said, moved. Then he said, "Thanks for lunch, and it was nice to meet you. I'll be going now; I need to get busy earning my keep around here. Will it disturb anybody if I mow the lawn near the back of the house?"

"Nobody here but me and Billy and Dash. I got clothes to wash and probably won't even hear the mower, and the boys are supposed to rehearse, so it won't bother them."

"Rehearse?"

"Yes. That string group I mentioned. They rehearse here just about every afternoon. Sometimes downstairs in the study, but usually upstairs in the music room. It's classical music. Do you like that kind of music?"

John Henry smiled. "Don't know a lot about it, but I seem to like all kinds of music, not just rock 'n' roll. Pop. Jazz. Big band. Swing. Dixieland. Even some country music, but a little of that goes a long way. But, now, when it's people like Frank Sinatra and Duke Ellington doing their thing, I could listen all day."

"No gospel."

"Yeah, even some of that." He grinned. "I grew up hurryin' to catch that heaven-bound train that Sister Wynona Carr was always singing about."

Immediately, Henrietta showed that she knew the song well. Doing a little shuffle by the kitchen sink, she broke out singing, delighting John Henry with her rhythmic moves and contralto vocalizing: "...*Hey, Lord, I said don't miss that tr-ay-ay-ay-ay-ain. Don't miss that tr-ay-ay-ay-ay-ain*...."

"Ha!" he exclaimed, laughing, clapping his hands, and dancing with glee. "That sounds just like her. You got her down pat." He pointed to Henrietta's slippered feet. "Yo' footwork ain't bad, either, girl. How old did you say you were?"

Henrietta's brown face flushed. "Forty-nine," she said. "I was joshin' you when I said fifty-two." She gave him a look that dared him to register doubt.

37

"Forty-nine!" he said with a great show of surprise. "I took you for much younger."

Henrietta smiled victoriously and John Henry went on out. Two minutes later she heard the lawn-mower engine roar to life.

Chapter Three

OCCASIONALLY in mowing, John Henry had to turn off the engine to move a stick or other obstruction in the mower's path or take a sip of water. Each time he did, he heard music – sometimes a guitar and piano, sometimes a guitar and bass. Evidently, Billy was teaching Dash the tunes he had learned just that morning. And already they were sounding pretty good on them.

He stood listening for a moment as the familiar bass introduction to "Mustang Sally" throbbed over the back lawn: *DUM, dum-dum-dum; DUM, dum-dum-dum.* John Henry smiled: *That boy might not be able to talk for hisself, but he sure can make that bass talk.* "Yes, sir!" John

Henry told himself. "You could hang clothes out to dry on that bass line."

He fired up the mower again and set off across the wide lawn with Wilson Pickett's vocal echoing in his mind. It put a little bounce in his step. ". . .*One of these early mornings, gonna put yo' flat feet on the ground . . . .*"

An hour or so later, when John Henry had finished the mowing and was putting away the lawn mower, he saw a car pull into the driveway and park. Soon six young people, three guys and three girls, got out and began unloading musical instruments. Hoping to hear them rehearse, John Henry went to his apartment, washed up, and poured himself a glass of ginger ale. Then, picking up the morning newspaper, which he had not yet finished reading, he went out onto his small balcony and sat.

For awhile, all he heard were the sounds of instruments tuning up, so he sipped his cool drink and concentrated on the sports pages of *The Atlanta Constitution*. But when the sounds indicated that the players were about to begin in earnest, he put down the paper to listen. The sounds seemed to be coming from a downstairs room near the end of the wing he faced. Probably the study, he thought. Through the room's open windows – the kind that crank out – he could see books and bookshelves, and shadows that occasionally flickered on the window panes.

Then, as if by magic, full, rich, orchestral music swelled suddenly into the afternoon like a rapturous incantation. It came so suddenly and so unexpectedly that John Henry nearly dropped his ginger ale. *My God!* he thought; *they sound professional!* At first, he didn't recognize the tune. His knowledge of classical music was limited. But this had to be Bach, didn't it? Yes. He was sure. Something by Bach for the cello, which, as he listened, filled the air with sounds so voluptuous that he thought of them first as the blooming of flowers set to music, and then as a lyrical measuring of life itself.

Wow, he thought. *Those kids can sho' nuff play!* Whoever was playing the cello was interpreting each line with a sensitivity that John Henry had heard only in jazz musicians. And was that Dash on the piano? What a touch he had! And the bass and drums seemed to spread the perfect canvas on which the melody could paint.

Later, long after the rehearsal had ended, John Henry sat in a lawn chair just inside one bay of the four-car garage. He had set up there to be out of the sun while he checked various garden tools, sharpening the blades on some, tightening loose screws on others, and, at the moment, cleaning the spark plug of a leaf blower. On the concrete floor at his side was a small record player and a stack of old 45's. The sound was low, but it must have carried on the still, June air, for suddenly John Henry realized that he had company: Billy and Dash.

"Who's that on the saxophone?" Billy asked, pointing to the colorful little record spinning on the small record player. Dash stood back and slightly behind Billy.

"Junior Walker," John Henry said. "The group is Junior Walker & the All Stars. The tune is called 'Shotgun.'"

Billy turned to Dash. "Sonny's got to hear that." Dash made no sign of recognition. Billy turned to John Henry. "Sonny's our horn man. One of 'em. The main one."

John Henry smiled. "Bring him around. The more, the merrier."

The record ended and another dropped onto the turntable and began spinning. This time, out of a noisy downbeat that sounded not unlike the dropping of pots and pans, the block chords of an inspired piano filled the garage.

John Henry saw rapt attention animate Dash's face, and Billy began swaying slightly to the sound. Then, when the voice of Marvin Gaye broke through, using the piano chords as a counterpoint to a soulful lament, John Henry began to sing along under his breath. ". . .*I know flowers grow from rain, but how can love grow from pain? Ain't that peculiar? Ain't that peculiar?*"

Throughout the playing of the record, Billy and Dash inched closer and closer to the machine. When the music stopped, Dash looked at John Henry and pointed at the record, a question brimming behind his eyes. He extended his hands and flexed the fingers of both.

John Henry laughed. "You mean the piano player?"

Dash nodded yes.

"I don't know, but he's a playin' fool, ain't he?" John Henry had always liked especially the apparent wild abandonment of this record. The pianist did not seem so much to be playing back-up to Marvin Gaye as building his own interpretation of the lyrics, which to John Henry were among the most inventive in all of Rock 'n' Roll. And the overall impression was of hearing two distinct versions of the same song that nonetheless meshed perfectly through some alchemy of the poetry of pain.

"Holy Moses!" Billy said quietly. "We've never heard nobody play like that before."

"Anybody," John Henry corrected.

"Naw," Billy said, agreeing, not understanding that his grammar was being corrected.

When the next record plopped onto the turntable, Billy and Dash both leaned still closer to the machine as if eager to see what magic the little box would serve up next. When a slightly raspy voice with cutting-edge clarity began strutting through "Papa's Got a Brand New

Bag," Billy, beside himself with joy at the music, began to dance around the garage.

Dash watched with a big smile on his face, his knees flexing to the funky rhythm.

"Who's that?" Billy called.

"James Brown. The Godfather of Soul." John Henry was feeling the rhythm, too, tapping a foot, nodding his head.

Billy beamed. "I like him." To Dash he called, "Listen to *those* horns."

Trumpets playing in perfect unison punctuated the vocal with what sounded like joyous affirmation.

"Wow," said Billy. "And listen to that guitar!"

Dash pointed and grunted as the record ended.

John Henry guessed that he wanted to know what was next. But before he could answer that he wasn't sure, a slow, voluptuous piano and bass introduction rose sinuously from the record player, to be followed by a rich contralto voice seething with sensuality.

"Aretha Franklin," John Henry noted. "Baby, I Love You."

Billy stopped dancing around the garage and stood still to listen. Dash, his mouth slightly open, his eyes wide, his body swaying, looked as if he might be in a trance. And when the horns began to play, as if commenting sympathetically on the singer's smouldering testimony of love, Dash looked as if he might swoon. Watching him, John Henry smiled broadly and thought: *That boy's heart might be broken, but ain't nuthin' wrong with his soul.* Then he leaned back to listen more closely. *". . . Told you once, little boy, you know you got it; I'd deny my own self before I'd see you without it, 'cause I love you. . ."*

"Wow, can she sing!" Billy said as the record ended. "What band is that?"

"Just studio musicians," John Henry said. "But they sure were cooking that day."

At first, Billy and Dash looked confused by what John Henry had said. But then they smiled. "That's a good way to put it," Billy said: "cooking."

Dash laughed and nodded.

"Got anything else by them?" Billy asked.

As he spoke, the introduction to "Chain of Fools" sounded.

"See what you think of this one," John Henry said.

This number had a faster tempo, but the voice was the same — supercharged with emotion, fierce with anger, raw with pain. Then, roughly midway in the record, when the singer and musicians seemed to shift into overdrive, the hard-charging rhythm sent Billy bounding around the garage in even higher spirits than before, and now Dash hobbled after him, swaying and grinning as if in the grip of a delicious lunacy. ". . .*One of these mornings, the chain is gonna break . . ."* Aretha keened. Even John Henry, though still seated, was bouncing for joy, unable to sit still.

It was at that very moment that a white Lincoln Continental appeared suddenly at the garage entrance, the whir of the engine drowning out the music, heat from the engine surging into the garage. The driver's door opened and Billy's father stepped out onto the parking apron, his face saying clearly that he did not approve of the antics he had come upon. Looking stern, he stood looking first at Billy, then at Dash, and then at John Henry, who felt he could see Mr. Randolph putting the parts of the scenario together in his head and not liking the tableau at all. Not one little bit.

The two boys looked frozen in place, as if they had been playing a child's game that flung them into abandoned postures they were supposed to hold until the game was over. John Henry, hoping to appear the picture of innocence, smiled at Mr. Randolph and then studied the spark plug he had been cleaning desultorily as if it were now the most fascinating object he had ever beheld and perhaps the dirtiest. He lofted a silent prayer of thanks that "Chain of Fools" had been the last record on the turntable and that the garage was now quiet.

"Billy, go inside," Mr. Randolph said. "You, too, Dash."

The boys trooped out the door and toward the house, scurrying like scolded puppies.

Mr. Randolph then stood looking at John Henry, or so John Henry thought as he wilted under the gaze. But then Mr. Randolph turned and walked into the house.

John Henry heaved a sigh of relief and sent heavenward an addendum to his earlier prayer: *Thanks. Again. I owe You. Again.*

Chapter Four

"**W**HAT DID he say?" Henrietta was rinsing breakfast dishes and putting them into the dishwasher.

John Henry was telling her about Mr. Randolph's sudden appearance and baleful look the day before. "Nothin'. Didn't have to." John Henry sipped from a cup of coffee. "I felt about *that* small." He held up his right hand, showing maybe half an inch between thumb and index finger. After a moment, he asked, "Did I get the boys in trouble?"

"Mr. Randolph didn't say nothin' to me, and I can read Dash like a book. He was okay, too." She turned and looked across the kitchen at John Henry, seated in the breakfast area. "Don't think nothin' of it. Mr. Randolph got a

52

lot bigger worries than what Billy and Dash might be up to. I ain't seen him smile in a month of Sundays, and that's the truth."

"Business worries, I hear."

"Yeah. He don't talk to me about 'em, but I hear things. He got five radio stations, and none of 'em is doing as good as he think they ought to."

"Are they all like WSOF? Same format, I mean?"

"No. One is all sports. One is all talk. One, in Texas, is aimed at Mexicans and Americans. Tex-Mex, I think they call it. One in California is soft music, though, same as WSOF. Ain't none of 'em got the ratings he wants 'em to have."

"No oldies?"

"Just you and me," Henrietta said, smiling, surprising John Henry with her sly wit.

He laughed. "Nothin' wrong with *your* ratings," he said, "at least in my book."

Laughing, Henrietta turned from the sink and put her hands on her hips. "Now ain't you nice? Must be getting ready to hit me up for a loan."

He looked wounded and raised both hands as if to shield himself from such low suspicion. "No, no." Then he composed a face of angelic innocence. "It's just my natural-born honesty speaking: in other words, I cannot tell a lie."

"I can't either," Henrietta said extravagantly: "You full of bull!"

They laughed so hard that John Henry splashed coffee from his cup, and Henrietta had to sit down to keep from falling down. She slumped into a chair next to his.

After the fit of laughter, they fell quiet for a few moments, and then out of nowhere Henrietta said with a long face, "Tell you who better not hear Billy and Dash playin' no rock 'n' roll."

54

"Who? Mrs. Randolph?"

Henrietta waved a hand. "Nah. She easy to get along with. A real lady. No, I was thinkin' of the boys' music teacher, Clair Montrose."

"Woman?"

"Man. He thinks they ain't been no new music since Beethoven and his classical buddies died off."

"One of those, eh?"

"Yeah."

John Henry chuckled. "Guess he wasn't listening when ol' Chuck Berry told Beethoven to 'roll over and tell Tchaikovsky the news.'"

Henrietta laughed. "Well, everybody else heard him! The *whole world* heard him!"

"Ain't *that* the truth. You could make a case that Chuck Berry was the Paul Revere of rock 'n' roll."

"On a guitar, though, 'stead of a horse."

Again John Henry, laughing, was impressed by Henrietta's quick wit. "And him a *black*smith instead of a silversmith," he added.

His own quickness caught Henrietta by surprise, and when she exploded in a gale of laughter John Henry did, too, each collapsing against the other's shoulder in a helpless surrender to mirth.

When their laughter was spent and they had composed themselves again, John Henry sat up straight and said, "What is this recital the boys have coming up?"

"Well, I said recital 'cause I didn't know what else to call it. But it's for the Atlanta Arts Festival. That's a big event held every year in Piedmont Park, in downtown Atlanta. Lasts two or three days and features lots of arts and crafts shows, and musical performances of all kinds – different ones on different days."

"I've seen that park. It's a big, big park."

"Well, it'll be filled with a sea of people next month. I'd go if it was just to people-watch, but I enjoy the shows and displays, too. And it's a real honor for Billy and Dash and the other kids to be invited to perform there. They drew a good day, too: Saturday."

John Henry gave Henrietta a pointed look. "I heard 'em rehearsing yesterday; they're good enough to play *anywhere*."

They fell silent again for a moment, but at length Henrietta said, "I honestly don't know what would have become of Dash if he hadn't discovered music. He was one sad and lost little boy until he met up with the piano, the one in the music room." She nodded toward the wing of the house that held that room. "Just sat down one day and started to play. Completely natural. Surprised us all. Then come to find out he could play most any instrument by ear."

John Henry nodded. "It's a gift. Erroll Garner played by ear, too—"

"Who?"

"Erroll Garner. Black man. Jazz pianist. Died years ago – but, man, could he play! Like I said: It's a gift."

Henrietta sighed. "Yeah. But in Dash's case it was more like a blessing. The way I see it, the Devil took his momma, so to make up for it God gave him the next best thing: music."

John Henry looked searchingly at Henrietta for a long moment. "I sure do like the way you think, lady – but I believe this time you're wrong. God gave him *you*, Henrietta. He sho' nuff did. *You're* the real blessing in that boy's life."

Moved, Henrietta bit her lip and made no reply, and for a moment John Henry thought she might cry. Instead she heaved a great sigh and said, "Maybe so." Then shooting a sly glance at John Henry, she erupted in laughter and added, "'Cause he sho' know how to play *me*, too."

Taken aback at first, John Henry soon joined her in a gale of laughter, slapping the table repeatedly in a paroxysm of mirth as Henrietta laughed and cried at the same time. They recovered their composure only when Mrs. Randolph, dressed to go out, entered the kitchen to ask Henrietta to call an electrician.

"Something's wrong with their microphone. Or maybe it's one of the loudspeakers," Mrs. Randolph said. "They're rehearsing with all that electronic stuff this morning because they'll need it at the arts festival. I'd call, myself, but I'm late for my hair appointment."

Henrietta started to rise, but John Henry stayed her with a hand on her forearm and got up, himself. To Mrs. Randolph, he said, "Mind if I have a look? I've had some experience with microphones and such."

"The music room is in the east wing, upstairs, end of the hall," Mrs. Randolph said, smiling and pointing the general direction. "Thank you."

Chapter Five

"THE MICROPHONE plug is fine, so it must be *here*." John Henry was now examining the outlet that Billy had been trying to use. He turned the switch on a lamp that was plugged into the outlet. No light came on. "Got a screwdriver handy?" he asked. Billy offered to fetch one, but John Henry said, "Never mind. I think I can get to this with my pocket knife."

Moments later, he inserted the microphone's plug into the outlet, and the hum of a live mike filled the room.

Billy, who was strumming on his guitar, heard the hum, and grinned at John Henry. "Hey, thanks," he said.

Dash looked up from the piano, where he had been doodling with blues chords. He grinned, too.

Billy then caught Dash's eye. Looking conspiratorial, he smiled and said, "Let's show him."

Dash nodded, jumped up from the piano, and picked up a bass guitar as Billy, hunched over his own guitar, began to play and then sing: *"One night with you is what I'm now waitin' for. . ."*

John Henry's smile lit up the room. "You sound just like him!" he called out.

Billy didn't, not really, sound like Elvis; John Henry knew that. For one thing, the voice was too young. Still it was a very good emulation — every bit as soulful and love sick as Elvis himself sounded on that early recording, when one could easily picture him, down there in Tupelo, Mississippi, before his career began, doggedly practicing this song and its chords in

63

his bedroom at night while dreaming of performing on stage.

Giving a nod of thanks, Billy continued playing and singing: ". . .*now I know that life without you has been too lonely too long. . .*"

Clowning around, Dash grinned and punctuated the break in the lyrics with some booming bass notes, comedic but melodically fitting, too.

Spying a drum set he hadn't noticed before, John Henry held up a hand to indicate that he was going to join in. In no time, it seemed, he was seated behind the drums and wielding brushes he had found there to lay down subtle, supporting licks. Playing together smoothly, joyously, the three went through the song one more time and then rolled to a rousing finish with Billy wailing the last words ". . .*would make my dream come trueeee.*"

A burst of applause caught the trio by surprise. The other members of the octet had arrived for practice. Applauding with them was Henrietta, who had shown the newcomers in.

Beaming, Henrietta called, "I didn't know you could play the drums, John Henry. You full of surprises."

"I *can't* play the drums," John Henry insisted, blushing. "Anybody who *can* play would *tell* you I can't."

"Well, you sure fooled me," said Rich, who played drums in the high school band. "That was a great number! What was it?"

"Yeah!" the other musicians exclaimed. Moving on into the room, they huddled around Billy and Dash and John Henry.

"Where'd you learn that?" said Angela Ashford. A shapely black girl of about age sixteen, she touched Billy's shoulder to get his attention and said, "Teach me that song." Angela played keyboards and the violin, and she also sang in her church's choir.

"OK," Billy said. Directing his gaze at John Henry, he told her, "I learned it from him – or, rather, from a record he's got. He's got lots of 'em. Great stuff, too. Stuff I never heard before."

"What's a record?" Marcella Howard asked. Puzzlement played around her pretty face, which was framed by long black curls that cascaded down her back. In the octet, she mainly played cello, but she could also play piano and violin.

"Records were the things before tapes and CDs and MP3s came along," said Sonny Smith, a lanky sixteen-year-old. In the octet, he mostly played clarinet, but he could play just about any horn and was especially proficient on the saxophone. "Your parents probably have some old records stuck away in the attic. Mine do."

"Can we hear your records?" Barbara Coffman asked John Henry. "Where are they?"

"Yeah," said Clifford Claxton, a freckled redhead who also was about sixteen years old. "And this time let *me* play the bass," he said to Dash, who nodded agreement. Besides the bass guitar, Clifford played the trumpet and valve trombone, shining beyond his years on the Bach selections in the octet's repertoire.

"But don't y'all have to practice?" John Henry asked.

"Not yet," said Barbara, a cute blonde who was about Billy's age. She looked at her watch. It was nine-thirty. "We usually practice at this time, but Mr. Montrose phoned Henrietta to say he would be late. Car trouble."

When John Henry hesitated to reply, Billy said, "Please, John Henry, can we?" The same plea was written all over Dash's face as he closed ranks with Billy and looked eagerly at John Henry.

"We'll go get your record player," Billy offered. "Won't we, Dash?"

67

Dash grinned and nodded.

Johnny Henry shrugged his shoulders and gave in. "Ain't nobody said not to," he reasoned. "The player is still in the garage, right where we left it. Stack of records there, too."

Billy raced for the door, with Dash limping right behind him.

In no time at all, it seemed, the boys trooped back into the room, Billy carrying the little 45 rpm record player, Dash balancing a large stack of the little records with the big hole in the middle, and both boys proceeding as ceremonially as if their cargo were holy relics.

"Over here," Billy instructed Dash, nodding toward a table along a wall, near an electrical outlet. While Billy plugged in the record player and turned it on, Dash looked at John Henry and pointed to the stack of records, now on the table. *Which one?* he wanted to know.

John Henry smiled. "Any of 'em."

Dash selected one and put it on the turntable. Soon, the sound of violins swirled in the room, followed closely by a girl's plaintive voice: *"Your kisses tell me it's goodbye; my eyes know they're gonna cry..."*

Love those strings," Barbara said to no one in particular.

"Yeah, but *listen* to that girl sing," said Marcella as the vocalist spun out more of the song's lament: *". . .Our love's becoming a thing of the past. . ."*

"That's Shirley Owens," John Henry volunteered. "Lead singer of the Shirelles, one of the best girl groups ever."

"Never heard of her. Or them." A look of amazement played on Marcella's pretty face. "I wonder why."

John Henry smiled. "Way before your time, Miss. That song was big in, oh, 1960." He anticipated her next question and told her the

69

name of the tune. "'(Our Love's Becoming) A Thing of the Past.'"

"*Ooooh*, I like it," Marcella said. "Don't you, Barbara? Angela?"

Both girls nodded dreamily as they listened raptly and swayed to the music.

"I like her voice," Barbara said. "It's funky."

"I do, too," Marcella said. "And those lyrics!"

". . .*You used to call me your sugar-baby; now I say call me, you tell me maybe…* "

"Just like a guy!" Angela said, rolling her eyes and sighing as Barbara and Marcella made signs and faces of sad, heartfelt agreement.

With impeccable phrasing, Shirley Owens's voice, propelled by pain, anger, and heartbreak, sailed into the song's last few bars: ". . .*if you don't love me, stop pretending. Who needs a book with a heartbreak ending. . .?*"

"Oh!" Barbara and Angela gasped and collapsed against each other in a swoon of appreciation, and they readily agreed when Marcella said, "We've *got* to learn that song!" Turning to John Henry, Marcella wrung her hands and pleaded, "Can we borrow your record and player, pretty please? Can you leave it here so we can learn that song?"

"Sure. If it's all right with Billy. I've got another player back at my pad."

Billy nodded and said thanks as Dash dropped another record onto the turntable. Seconds after a rousing guitar downbeat, everybody in the room, even John Henry, was dancing or moving in some fashion to The Beatles' infectious tribute to teenage love, "I Saw Her Standing There."

"Wow! That song takes off like a race horse," Billy said as Paul McCartney, the lead singer on this selection, launched into his raw,

71

highly charged vocal, his voice lashed by driving guitar riffs and youthful hormones.

"Well, she was just seventeen, you know what I mean, and the way she looked was way beyond compare. . ."

"Oh, boy," Rich said. "A drummer could *really* get into music like that."

"Bass player, too," said Barbara, and Clifford nodded vigorously in agreement.

By the time McCartney reached the song's screeching juvenile declaration of love at first sight – *"...Well, my heart went boom when I crossed that room and I held her hand in mine..."* – everybody in the room was singing along in full-throated abandonment. They froze as one, however, when at the record's end the door to the room flew open and for an instant each of them thought that Mr. Montrose had arrived and caught them in mid-frolic. They nearly collapsed in relief when it registered on them that it was merely Henrietta who stood in the doorway.

She announced: "Mr. Montrose call again and say he prob'ly can't git here today, after all," and she was taken aback when all the young people cheered. Shaking her head in bemusement, she closed the door and went away again.

"Put on another record, Dash!" Marcella called, and soon all of them were caught up again in the primal energy and joyful exuberance of what John Henry called "that old-time rock 'n' roll."

On and on, till nearly lunchtime, they listened to this intoxicating music – and to John Henry's stories about it. He surprised even himself with the vast storehouse of essentially useless knowledge of popular music that he had accumulated over the years – tidbits about this or that recording artist, song, songwriter, or musician:

– "That's 'Baby I Love You,'" by Aretha Franklin, same gal you heard a minute ago doing 'Chain of Fools.' Memphis girl, daughter of a Baptist preacher. Known as the Queen of Soul for what critics called the 'scorching intensity' of her singing. She was big in the '60s and '70. Still around, too, last I heard.

– "The *King* of Soul? Well, maybe Ray Charles. You heard him a few minutes back, singing about drowning in his own tears. Great horns in there, remember? He was a Georgia boy. Albany. Blind. Played the piano. I first heard him in 1957 on the radio. He was singing 'Swanee River Rock,' and I knew when I heard him that a new day in rock 'n' roll had dawned. Stephen Foster's probably still spinning in his grave.

– "But maybe the King of Soul was Otis Redding, another Georgia boy, Macon. He was the one who wound up 'Sittin' on the Dock of the Bay' in San Francisco, defeated 'cause he couldn't satisfy all the people who were telling him what to do. I can identify with that feeling, can't you? Redding's the same man, by the way, who was telling people, on the record before that one, to call him 'Mr. Pitiful.' He was about as soulful as they come. Dead now.

— "But my personal vote for the King of Soul would have to be Marvin Gaye. That was him singing I 'Heard It on the Grapevine,' which always sounded to me like a suicide note set to music. Anyhow, that song became a sort of anthem of rock 'n' roll because all of us at one time or another have lost in love, been the last to know of a lover's betrayal, and thought the loss would surely kill us. And his performance on 'Ain't That Peculiar,' which all of you seemed to like a lot, is still another poem of tortured love by him that's in a class by itself because of his unique styling.

"Now, still another Macon, Georgia, treasure was a diamond in the rough named

Richard Penniman, who became known the world over as Little Richard. Clown Prince of Rock 'n' Roll might be a more fitting title for him than King of Soul because his music was happy and fun-loving instead of soulful. But whatever he was he was one of a kind – in other words, unique. His 'awop-bop-a-loo-mop-a-lop-bam-boom,' which y'all heard on 'Tutti Frutti," his first hit, put me in mind, when I first heard it, and it still does, of old Walt Whitman's famous line: 'I sound my barbaric yawp over the roof of the world.' Well, Little Richard sounded his own 'barbaric yawp,' and teenagers everywhere – I was one myself one time – heard it, and nothing's been the same since, at least not in popular music. He unleashed a wild something in music that hadn't been there before – not a dangerous wild, just an uninhibited one. He got big in the '50s, back when rock 'n' roll was still called rhythm and blues – and he's still around, still performing, I hear. Remember 'Good Golly Miss Molly?' Played a few minutes ago? Credence Clearwater Revival? Well, Little Richard wrote it – and It's been recorded by a zillion people since then – but the royalties went into somebody else's pocket. The story goes that when everything he was touching turned to gold, he sold the rights to that song for peanuts, about $60."

Suddenly a voice boomed from the doorway: "And that was fifty-nine dollars and 98 cents too much."

All heads turned toward the door. Mr. Montrose stood there, staring daggers at John Henry and obviously fuming. Henrietta stood behind him, giving John Henry a look of helplessness.

Mr. Montrose strode into the room. Looking from face to face among his students and pointing toward the record player, he said, "So *this* is how you spend rehearsal time when I'm not around." He paused. "Listening to rock 'n' roll. Junk music. Music for simpletons." He stared at John Henry. "'Barbaric yawp' is right, sir – Mister whoever-you-are."

Billy spoke. "That's John Henry."

From the doorway, Henrietta added meekly, "He works here."

Mr. Montrose walked over to the record player, now quiet, but turntable still turning. He turned to John Henry. "Is this your, uh, stuff?" His face was a sneer.

John Henry nodded.

"Out!" Mr. Montrose snapped. "Get it out of here. This is a *music* room, not a zoo!"

Billy spoke up. "It's my fault, Mr. Montrose. I asked him to play his records for us. He's my friend."

"Not for long, he isn't. Just wait till I speak to your father."

"It was my fault, not John Henry's," Billy said.

"They didn't mean any harm," Henrietta added. "They thought you wasn't comin.'"

"Good thing I did," Mr. Montrose said. "The arts festival is only two weeks away, and I find you wasting rehearsal time listening to trashy music. Billy, you know how your father feels about such popular trash."

John Henry unplugged his record player, gathered up his records, and left the room.

"All right now!" Mr. Montrose shouted. "Places everybody!"

The musicians scurried to their seats as Henrietta followed John Henry down the hallway and into the kitchen. "He just blew in while I was in the pantry," she said, pointing toward a door. "I didn't have a chance to warn y'all."

"I just hope I didn't get Billy and Dash in trouble."

"Well, he won't like it none, but I'll tell him you was just checkin' the outlet you fixed."

79

John Henry was flattered, but he fixed her with what he hoped was a stern look. "Don't go getting' in trouble on account of me, woman. I already got Billy and Dash on my conscience."

She stared back at him. "Didn't you fix that outlet?"

"Yes."

"How'd you know it was fixed?"

"I plugged in my record player and it worked."

"Ain't that what I said?"

John Henry shook his head and heaved a sigh. "I surrender."

"I accept." Henrietta turned away. "Now get out of my kitchen. I got too much to do to stand here talkin' to you all day."

"OK," John Henry said, "but I'd like to leave my player and records here. Billy and Dash wanted to borrow them."

"Here," Henrietta said, taking them from John Henry. "I'll just put them out of sight until Mr. Music Snob is gone."

Chapter Six

RIGHT AFTER lunch, John Henry, raking the yard on the far side of the house, saw Mr. Montrose come out the front door and walk to his car. But as the music teacher was about to get into the car, Mr. Randolph's Lincoln Continental pulled into the driveway and stopped when Mr. Montrose hailed him.

John Henry watched as Mr. Randolph put down the driver's-side window while Mr. Montrose hurried over to speak to him. They were out of John Henry's hearing range, but the music teacher's behavior was a crystal-clear pantomime of indignation and wrath, and John Henry had no doubt at all that he was the target of this tirade. Talking non-stop, Mr. Montrose pointed repeatedly toward the house while

slashing the air with first one hand and then the
other, and John Henry felt that he could even
guess the gist of Mr. Montrose's heated
declamation: *I caught that yardman of yours in
the act of corrupting your son and my whole octet by
exposing them to barbaric music – while they were
supposed to be rehearsing for the arts festival! I can
not teach under such conditions. Either he goes or I
go.*

John Henry, who had long ago stopped
raking, was partly obscured from sight by tall
shrubbery and tree branches, but now he edged
his way to the corner of the house and eased out
of sight altogether. He stood there, scarcely
breathing, until he heard the two men exchange
goodbyes, a car door slam, and engines revving.
He then went back to work, expecting at any
moment to be summoned to the house, called on
the carpet, and fired. But only a few minutes
later, he saw Mr. Randolph's car emerge from

the driveway and onto the street, and then drive away.

"*Whew!*" He let out a deep breath and began to rake in earnest. He didn't let himself jump to the conclusion that he was safe, but at least it was a stay of execution. Moments later, his thoughts now elsewhere, he grinned as he heard the familiar downbeat of "Bright Lights, Big City" emanating from an open window upstairs.

Soon, the song's strutting beat had John Henry raking with renewed energy, and even dancing from time to time with the rake as his partner, as the stuttering drums, the cascading notes of the guitar, Jimmy Reed's bluesy vocal, and then that awesome, wailing harmonica filled him with – what else could one call it? – joy, the sheer joy of feeling a delicious syncopation mesh perfectly with emotions elicited by the music: *"Bright lights, big city, gone to my baby's head. . .*

"

When the record ended, John Henry smiled as he heard Billy and his friends begin to practice some of the record's more pronounced riffs. He figured it was Rich on drums, but who was that on bass? Dash? And who on guitar? Billy? He heard no vocal, but again and again the youngsters practiced the song's opening until they had it just right. Damn, they were good, John Henry thought. *Picked it up in no time!*

Then, as he was putting away the rake, he heard from yet another open window the strains of one of his all-time favorite feel-good numbers: "Walkin' the Dog," by Rufus Thomas, another of rock 'n' roll's clown princes. A life-size picture popped into John Henry's head: Rufus wearing a cape and hamming it up for all he (and the song) was worth. Soon, the tune's wonderful, non-sensical, nursery-rhyme lyrics had John Henry retrieving his rake for another dance, this time around the spacious garage floor: *"Asked my mama for fifteen cents, see the elephant jump the fence. He jumped so high he touched the sky; never got back till the Fourth of July."*

No sooner had the record ended than John Henry heard the young musicians attempting to emulate the song's funky rhythms – and in no time at all, it seemed, they had the song's parts down pat. Somebody was even singing the lyrics – and not doing a bad job of it, at all! *Wish I was in there with 'em*, he thought. Even if he said so himself, he used to do a pretty good job of imitating ol' Rufus. Still had the cape stored away somewhere.

What surprised John Henry as much as the kids' talent, though, was how long and hard they practiced. He smiled, remembering that old joke: *"How do you get to Carnegie Hall?" "Practice, brother, practice!"* The youngsters were still at it at four o'clock when John Henry left to make a run to the grocery store. He had to force himself to get into his truck, because now the kids were rehearsing "Will You Still Love Me Tomorrow," another of the wonderful hit songs by the Shirelles. The girls' plaintive voices reached his ears. Was that Marcella singing the lead? No matter. Whoever it was had an amazing voice, crystal clear, and John Henry, profoundly impressed, waited for the very last note to fade before driving out of the yard.

For the next several days, John Henry checked often for Mr. Randolph's car and made sure not to cross paths with Mr. Montrose, who showed up every morning at 9:30 sharp for two hours of rehearsal. And every day, as soon as Mr. Montrose left, his classical string octet morphed into a rock 'n' roll band, and the rehearsing continued, the musicians breaking only for a quick lunch, which at Henrietta's insistance they ate, sitting down, in the kitchen, "like civilized folks."

87

Though welcome to join them for lunch, John Henry shied away from the house's interior; Mr. Randolph might pop in at any moment, and that was a meeting he did not look forward to.

"He won't be back till Sunday," Henrietta told him at length. "And by then, he and ol' man Montrose be done forgot about you."

Mr. Randolph, she said, was attending a bankers' convention in New York City "in hopes of gettin' another loan, I 'spect." She paused. "And all of us better pray he gits it."

"Things are that bad, eh?"

"Worse. I come up on Miz Randolph cryin' the other day."

"And she told you?"

"Didn't have to. I got ears, ain't I?" She turned away. Conversation over.

Mr. Randolph did get back to Atlanta on Sunday, as planned, but he didn't make it all the way home. Experiencing chest pains during the flight, he went straight from Hartsfield International Airport to the emergency room at Grady Memorial Hospital. There, the doctor told him that he was indeed having a heart attack.

"If you'd gone on home from the airport instead of coming here," the doctor told him, "chances are you would no longer be with us."

Mr. Randolph was promptly admitted to the hospital and placed in its intensive care unit, and Mrs. Randolph was summoned to his side.

"He bad off," Henrietta told John Henry the next day. "Doctor say he might not make it. Only thing to do now is pray."

Mr. Randolph teetered between life and death for three days and nights, during which time an almost palpable gloom hung over the Randolph residence, but the fourth day brought signs of recovery, a rally, and the gloom began to lift. Now, with the Piedmont Arts Festival only a few days away, the octet's two-a-day rehearsals resumed in earnest. July 4th, the festival's opening day, was just around the corner. Still, the group spent far more time playing rock 'n' roll than in rehearsing their classical program.

"We know those compositions backward and forward," Billy said. "It's the *new* stuff we want to learn."

Billy also insisted that John Henry join in their rock 'n' roll sessions, and all the others insisted, too – including Henrietta. .

"Tol' you not to worry," she said. "*I* run this house, and if I say I sent you to the music room, then to the music room you can go." She paused. "But wait till Mr. High 'n' Mighty Montrose leaves. No use invitin' trouble."

John Henry didn't have to be warned twice to avoid Mr. Montrose – or invited twice to join the youngsters as soon as Mr. Montrose left each day. He loved sitting in with them and soon was deeply involved in their practice sessions, even building his schedule of duties around their sessions when possible. The kids were loath to let him get away at all. They saw that he really knew music, knew a lot about performing, and was, for that matter, a much better musical director than Mr. Montrose would ever be, *could* ever be. John Henry's knowledge, enthusiasm, and personality made him a natural leader that they were eager to follow. Again and again, they worked to near-exhaustion, took a short break, and then went to work again – and all because they loved the music, music that, though new to them, was to John Henry simply that old time rock 'n' roll.

"Can't beat it," Henrietta would say after stopping by to listen for a while, something she now did often — to the detriment of her housework, she admitted ruefully to John Henry. She even took a turn at singing with them now and then.

"But what can they get for all this hard work?" she asked one day. "When do they go from rehearsin' this stuff to performing it?"

The question had never occurred to John Henry. After all, they weren't *his* octet, his band. He had just been fooling around and having a good time. But, no doubt about it, they were good enough now to play rock 'n' roll for an audience.

Henrietta's question now set him to thinking. "I don't know," he finally told her. "I'll have to think about it." To himself, he added silently: *If I'm still around after the arts festival.*

Chapter Seven

JULY THE FOURTH, a Saturday, first day of
the two-day Atlanta Arts Festival, dawned upon
the city with all the brilliance that a perfect
summer day in Georgia could bestow. The sun
shone brightly, a breeze from the nearby Blue
Ridge foothills moderated the customary heat,
and a powder-blue sky arched over the city like
a festive canopy, a few white clouds flying here
and there like banners.

With musical acts scheduled to begin at
11 a.m., Billy and the rest of the octet got to the
park an hour early to set up. John Henry drove
Billy there and stayed to help the group get
ready, but he steered a wide path around Mr.
Montrose, who was already on the scene,
barking orders left and right, and in general

making himself about as approachable as a rattlesnake.

The stage, owned by WSOF, was a mobile one with a sophisticated sound system and even an electric piano. Though the mobile unit's main purpose was for remote broadcasting, it was also used for live shows. Ideal for events such as the fair, it consisted of a covered flatbed trailer with retractable side panels so that the mobile unit could easily be transformed into stages of differing widths. Today, all the panels on one side had been removed, and atop the truck's open side, above the stage, stretched a banner proclaiming WSOF as "Your Number 1 Station for Music Worth Hearing."

After unloading chairs, music stands, and audio equipment from his pickup truck, John Henry rigged the sound system, conducted a sound check, and then returned home to do some chores before coming back with Henrietta around noon to hear the octet perform. Tearfully, Mrs. Randolph had excused herself from attending the fair so she could spend the time at the hospital with her husband, whose condition still was serious. Billy had offered to skip the fair and go to the hospital with her. He wasn't absolutely needed in the octet, he reasoned; it could easily morph into a septet. But Mrs. Randolph insisted that he go to the fair. His father, she said, would want him to honor his commitment to Mr. Montrose's group, as well as the radio station's commitment to the fair.

"That is one big park," John Henry announced to Henrietta when he got back home.

"Nearly 250 acres, they tell me," she said. "A green oasis smack dab in the heart of the city."

"And people everywhere you look already. A regular Pharaoh's army."

"Let's eat lunch early and then go," she said.

"Suits me fine."

"I sure hope the kids do well."

"No reason to worry about *them*. They are *good!*"

But, as it turned out, there *was* a reason to worry about them, a big reason: Nobody was listening to them. People were streaming by in the hundreds, but no one was stopping to hear them play. No one.

Under a big oak tree near the WSOF tent, John Henry set up folding chairs for himself and Henrietta, who had brought along a cooler containing sandwiches, ice, and tea. But they were the only spectators listening as the group played the sonorous but sprightly "Septet in E-flat major, Op. 20," by Beethoven, featuring Billy and Barbara on violins and

Sonny on the clarinet, while Rich sat this one out, as the piece required no percussion.

Sipping tea, Henrietta frowned as fairgoers, one after another, walked past without so much as a sidelong glance at the young musicians. "They must be deaf," she said. "That piece they're playing is beautiful."

John Henry agreed.

"Maybe it's just too early in the day for soft music," she added.

Or maybe it's too late *in the day, no matter how beautiful,* John Henry thought with irony, reflecting how times had changed since Beethoven's day. Curious, ever curious, John Henry had read up just last night on the octet's program, and he recalled that this particular piece dated back to 1800. *Two hundred and some-odd years ago!* No wonder *nothing* in the piece suggested the noise, the dissonance, the accelerated pace of modern times – all of which, he supposed, was a great part of its charm. But its proper setting, he thought, was the drawing room, or the concert hall, where one could feel insulated from the tumult of urban life. And it should occur in the evening, not at high noon. And in front of the appropriate audience, not the everyday listener whose musical appreciation rarely extended to Beethoven. *Chuck Berry was right,* he thought. *In fact, you could say he was* the *Paul Revere of rock 'n' roll, singing: "Roll Over, Beethoven, and tell Tchaikovsky the news. . ."*

During a break, Billy joined John Henry and Henrietta, and it was clear that he was very disappointed at being ignored by the crowd. "Besides you two, we've had only one other person as an audience — and it turned out that he was deaf and couldn't hear us anyhow. When I tried to ask if he had a special request, I saw that he wore a hearing aid and apparently had it turned down. He never answered."

Henrietta asked, "Well, is anybody here drawing a crowd?"

Billy pointed. "They're on break now, but when they're playing, everybody seems to be over there."

"Over there," when John Henry investigated, turned out to be a stage featuring rap performers. It was located about a hundred yards away from the WSOF tent, and its stage faced the stage on which Billy and his octet performed – but the contrast was striking. While the octet had no audience at all, except for Henrietta, a throng of people, mostly teenagers, milled about the rappers' tent, evidently waiting for the performers' break to end. The rappers were the hit of the festival, it seemed, and when their break was over, the throng moved as one to the front of their stage.

From a distance, John Henry watched the rappers for a while, trying to figure out why they were so popular with festival-goers, but after a half hour of watching, he declared himself mystified. The performers were not talented, even by rap standards as he understood them; the words, as usual in rap, were poorly rhymed, coarse, negative, often obscene, and wholly unimaginative; and all three of the rappers he had seen so far used the same, the very same, mannerisms and movements, all of them basic and wooden. And he neither saw nor heard a spark of originality from any of the performers, including the rhythm section backing the rappers, or hip-hoppers, or whatever they called themselves.

True, he noted, most of the audience were, like the performers, young African-Americans, and young people everywhere, he believed, were far more interested in feeling included in whatever was popular with their peers than in exhibiting discriminating tastes that might set them apart. He knew, too, that each generation generated its own music, which it likes even more if older folk don't.

But that was just it: What he was hearing wasn't music! He was sure of it. It was, if anything, theatre. A kind of socio-political theatre. Which might, in a limited way, be all well and good at certain times in certain places. But how on earth could this stuff – trashy talk against a rhythmic background – satisfy young people, or anybody, as a substitute for real music? He himself had been young once, hadn't he? The music of his youth had made him want to move! It went straight from his ears to his feet! OK, sometimes to his groin, too, but at least it was visceral, not cerebral, which rap pretended to be, purported to be, aspired to be, mistaking doggerel and juvenile brattiness for philosophy.

When the fifth rapper came onstage looking like a clone of the preceding four – baggy clothes, same awkward mannerisms,

101

amateurish stage presence, "lyrics" featuring "ho," "bitch," "fuck," and the like, and calling out the clichéd "Get yo' hands together" and "Give it up" — John Henry decided to "give it up" in his own way: He moved on. Over the next hour, he made a complete circuit of the park, stopping here and there, to see what other acts offered competition to Billy's octet. A country-music act had drawn a decent crowd. So had a Dixieland jazz band. A puppet show with organ-grinder music had attracted a flock of excited children, and not much farther on was a bluegrass group that was performing before a respectable number of people.

"The only musical competition I saw was the rappers," John Henry told Henrietta when he rejoined her. Finger-writing on air, he put "musical" in quotes to show Henrietta what he thought of it. He knew she shared his low opinion of rap. "People seem mostly interested in all the tents that feature arts and crafts," he added.

"Don't forget the food," Henrietta prompted. "Everybody who walks by here seems to be carrying food. And look over yonder," She pointed to a food wagon, the kind one sees at fairgrounds. "Look at 'em lined up for hot dogs and French fries. You'd think they'd never had a hot dog before today."

"Well, it's a festive occasion," John Henry said. But then he looked in the direction of Billy's tent. "Except over here," he added.

Henrietta nodded. "Still ain't nobody listenin'." She shook her head. "And those children practiced *sooo* hard."

By five o'clock, when the octet broke for an hour for supper, a very disconsolate group of young musicians sat around a picnic table that Henrietta had commandeered near the WSOF tent. They were dining on fair food fetched from a nearby barbecue stand as WSOF music, piped from the station, wafted from the tent's speakers – and again no one appeared to be listening.

"I counted about eighty people who stopped to hear us," Barbara said, frowning. "Eighty!"

"And there must be ten thousand people here," said Rich.

"Oh, more," said Sonny. "I saw people everywhere I looked."

"Except at our tent," Billy said with a sour look.

"Could it be our location?" Marcella asked.

"Oh, sure," said Rich, the word drenched in sarcasm.

Clifford lamented, "Where is Mr. Montrose when we need him?"

"Speak for yourself," Billy said.

"He left long ago," said Henrietta. "said he had to get back to the station."

Billy turned to John Henry, who was washing down the last of his second sandwich with a big drink of iced tea. "You know show business, John Henry. Any ideas?"

John Henry sighed. "Well, when I was breaking into show biz, I learned in a hurry to give folks what they wanted instead of what I wanted 'em to have."

"But what is it they want?" Barbara asked. "Rap?" They all turned to see in the distance people crowded around the rappers' stage. "We don't do rap."

"Don't *wanna* do rap," Sonny said.

"No, but you can do something a whole lot better than rap," John Henry said.

"What could be better than Beethoven?" Barbara asked, still thinking in terms of classical music.

John Henry smiled. "Remember that Chuck Berry tune y'all rehearsed?"

She nodded.

105

"A line in that song, from 1956, became the rallying cry of youngsters throughout the Western world," he said. "No offense to Mr. Ludwig Beethoven, but—"

"I know!" Billy shouted, beaming. "It was *'Roll over, Beethoven, and tell Tchaikovsky the news.'*"

"That's it!" John Henry said.

For a moment, nobody said anything. They simply looked at each other. It was as if all were thinking the unthinkable, but afraid to give it voice.

Billy finally spoke to the other musicians. "Are y'all thinking what I'm thinking?"

They shouted in unison: "Yes!"

Not sure what was afoot, Henrietta demanded, "Now what you up to, Billy boy?"

Billy looked her in the eye. "What I'm up to, Henrietta, is some rock 'n' roll. I'm tired of playing to nothing but the trees and sky, and what's going on here can't be good for the reputation of WSOF. He looked at the other members of the octet. "Are you with me?"

A chorus of "Yes" answered his question.

"Now, Billy," Henrietta cautioned. "Mr. Montrose will throw a fit."

Billy drew himself up to his full five feet, ten inches: "What's happening here is a dismal failure for all involved. My father's in no position, or condition, to decide what to do about it, so *I'll* do the deciding."

"John Henry," said Henrietta in an appeal for his help in reigning Billy in. But John Henry shook his head, no. "I think Billy's right," he told her.

"But his daddy don't like rock 'n' roll," she said.

"Well, we won't play loud enough for him to hear it," said Billy. He turned to John Henry. "Will you help us? We'll need Rich's drums and my guitar from the music room."

"I'm halfway home already," said John Henry, heading for his truck.

Chapter Eight

WHEN JOHN Henry backed his truck from the park's service road to the mobile stage, the octet was performing the beautiful "Octet Sonata," by Oliver Griswold – but to an audience of only three or four. When the players finished the number, Billy promptly announced an intermission, and went to the truck to fetch his guitar and amplifier. Rich and John Henry unloaded the drums, and Dash helped them set them up. John Henry had also fetched a bass guitar from the music room, just in case.

The other musicians moved aside all the chairs onstage. As a classical octet, they had performed while seated in a horseshoe formation. Now, except for Rich at the drums and Dash sometimes at the keyboards, they would play while standing. In half an hour the transformation was complete and the intermission was over.

Billy, standing stage center, eager to get started anew, asked John Henry, "What should we open with?"

John Henry, who was checking the microphone one last time, thought for a moment. "A Beatles number: 'I Saw Her Standing There.' If that doesn't pull people in, nothing will." He tapped on the mike. It was live. He backed away. "It's ready."

Billy smiled, called out the title to the others onstage, turned to the mike, and began shouting the song's familiar opening: "'One, two, three, four. . .'"

From the edge of the stage, John Henry watched as Rich, on the drums, laid down a driving rhythmic foundation for Barbara's bass, and for Billy's lead guitar and vocal. *No doubt about it*, John Henry thought; *these kids can play!* Their youthful energy matched that of the Beatles, he thought, and Dash, taking a turn on rhythm guitar because the song featured no piano, really cut loose on the bridge. Before he finished, John Henry saw festival patrons begin to gravitate toward the stage. By the time the number was over, a knot of people, maybe twenty or more, stood near the front of the stage.

Billy took a bow to good applause and pointed to each member of the band to share the applause with them. He then backed away from the mike to announce softly to the band: "Let's do 'One Night With You.'" Turning back to the microphone, Billy began to strum the guitar and sing in a raw, impassioned voice: *"One night with you is what I'm now praying for. . ."*

John Henry turned to Henrietta, who had joined him near the stage. "He's 'specially good on this one."

Henrietta nodded her agreement and listened closely. The song was little more than a vocal of scalding need sung against a backdrop of simple, stuttering drums and very elemental guitar- picking. But by the time the last notes of the Elvis tune rose to its familiar crescendo of primal need, an audience of more than a hundred had gathered in front of the stage, and they expressed their appreciation in spirited applause.

John Henry looked at Henrietta and beamed. "The boy can sing! He surely can."

"And him only fifteen!" she said.

John Henry nudged her with his elbow and winked at her: "Fifteen and a half."

Henrietta laughed and then, pointing toward the stage, said, "Look."

Now Marcella, Angela, and Barbara, holding their violins, had stepped forward, and stood before the microphone, poised to play. Standing slightly behind them, Billy readied his own violin, and behind him stood Dash, almost dwarfed by a big upright bass. A hush fell over the crowd, which now appeared to John Henry to be twice as large as before, with more people streaming across the park, heading their way.

Speaking into the mike, Marcella said softly, "And now a tribute to one of the greatest girl groups ever to make records: The Shirelles."

Seconds later, the familiar opening of "A Thing of the Past," featuring a cadenza of violins, swirled into the night as the slightly husky voice of Marcella, backed up by Angela and Barbara, slipped into the song's sad, sad lyrics: *"Your kisses tell me it's goodbye; my eyes know they're gonna cry. I feel I'm losing you too fast. Our love's becoming a thing of the past. . ."*

People standing in front of the stage began to sway with the music, and soon the whole audience swayed with them. Off to the side, stage right, a few couples began to dance.

113

At the song's end, the crowd yelled, "More! More!"

The girls looked to Billy for a suggestion. "Do 'Dancing in the Street,'" he said. "I think this audience is ready to roll."

The girls nodded. Billy turned to the other band members to tell them which number to play. Dash handed off the big bass to Sonny and moved to the keyboards, Barbara swapped her violin for the bass guitar, and Angela fetched a tambourine from somewhere stage right. Billy nodded to Barbara and Sonny, and both of them began to lay down a simple and solid bass line, with Dash shadowing each of their notes with bass notes from the piano. Next, Billy plunged in with blistering guitar chords, Angela began to bang the tambourine on her hip, and Marcella, propelled by Rich's drumming, launched into the lyrics: *"Calling out around the world, are you ready for a brand new beat. . ."* Before she even got to the next line, *". . .summer's here and the*

114

time is right for dancin' in the street. . ." the whole crowd, it seemed – and by now it *was* a crowd – began to writhe with the song's infectious rhythm, and many of them erupted in spontaneous dance.

John Henry leaned close to Henrietta's ear. "I think this song should be declared the national anthem of rock 'n' roll."

She leaned close to answer. "By Martha and the Vandellas or by the Mamas and the Papas?"

"Both are so good, it's too close to call," John Henry replied. "And Marcella's not doing bad with it, either."

Indeed she wasn't. As if feeding off her audience's enthusiasm, Marcella had plucked the center-stage mike from its stand and begun to do a few dance steps as she sang. This, in turn, made the crowd even more enthusiastic, and they began to sing with her: *". . .they're dancin' in Chicago, down in New Orleans, up in New York City. All we need is music, sweet music. . ."*

And as they sang and danced, the crowd grew and grew. Looking out over the park, John Henry saw people coming from every direction toward the source of the music they were hearing. He noticed also that only a few people now stood near the rappers' stage, though he could see that a performance was in progress there.

Henrietta had noticed, too, and nudged John Henry to look.

He leaned close to her ear. "Happy music beats crappy music every time."

She laughed and began applauding vigorously as Marcella's song ended. "Does this make you miss your performing days?" she asked John Henry.

He smiled. "Well, to be honest, yes, it does."

"Then get out there and do a number with 'em." She signaled to Billy by holding a downward-pointing finger over John Henry's head.

John Henry recoiled in mock horror. "What you up to, woman?"

Billy walked to the mike and said, "Ladies and gentlemen, please welcome our special guest, here from previous engagements in Las Vegas: the one and only John Henry Jones."

With that, Barbara on bass and Rich on drums began one of the most familiar openings in all of rock 'n' roll, the intro to "Mustang Sally": *DUM, dum-dum-dum; DUM, dum-dum-dum.* Henrietta gave John Henry a gentle push and he walked toward the microphone, shaking an accusing finger at Billy – but grinning, too; it had been a long time since he had been onstage, but it was soon clear to all that this man was no stranger to performing. With the crowd already swaying to the sustained rhythmic intro, John Henry grabbed the mike. Doing his best to emulate the legendary Wilson Pickett – grunts, primal screams, and all – he launched into the lyrics, giving the number everything he had. The crowd went wild. Henrietta stood just offstage, beaming. By the time John Henry reached the song's familiar chant of *"Ride, Sally, ride,"* the audience, in full throat, was singing it with him. The former classical octet – with Dash on the organ, Billy on lead guitar, Rich on drums, Clifford and Sonny playing saxophones, and the girls singing back-up – now sounded for all the world like a seasoned rock 'n' roll band.

When the audience demanded an encore, and the band and John Henry obliged, Barbara, Angela, and Marcella hurried to the wing at stage left and shanghaied Henrietta to join them in singing back-up. Henrietta offered resistance at first, but once she began to sing she felt right at home, and her voice added a new and rich dimension to the young girls' voices.

As the encore ended to vigorous applause by a still-swelling crowd chanting, "More! More!" John Henry took bow after bow, but the audience was reluctant to let him leave the stage. He looked at Billy helplessly and gave him a look that said "What now?" He got his answer when Billy and the band played some of the opening notes from Mendelssohn's "Wedding March." They were also the opening notes of one of John Henry's all-time favorite records, "Walking the Dog," by Rufus Thomas. To veteran ears, the beginning was a kind of musical bait-n-switch, announcing a classical tune only to dissolve into a funky beat featuring nursery rhymes, and propelled by a boiling guitar and a blistering bass. For a man of John Henry's talents and temperament, it was the perfect number to ham it up, and ham it up he did. Singing *"Mary Mack, dressed in black, silver buttons all down her back; high, low, tipsy- toe, she broke the needle and she can't sew. . . ,*" On the chorus, John Henry pretended to walk an invisible dog back and forth in front of the microphone. The audience howled in delight.

By the time the last notes of "Walking the Dog" were drowned in wild applause, the crowd listening to this former classical-music octet now numbered in the hundreds. Some guessed a thousand or more. Clearly, this no-name band of what many would have called "long-haired squares" was the festival's biggest draw. But with no pre-arranged program and the crowd yelling for more of the same, they were for a moment perplexed.

It was John Henry, with his old showman's experience, who sensed that a slower tempo was needed – but that it had to be one that wouldn't dampen the crowd's enthusiasm. First he whispered a suggestion to Billy, who passed the word to the other band members.

The intro to some songs is so good and so familiar to listeners everywhere that the first few notes spark recognition and generate an air of delicious anticipation. "Baby, I Love You," by Aretha Franklin, is one of those songs, and when Billy sent those first famous guitar notes boiling into the night, while Rich's drums and Dash's bass laid down a virtual walkway for the melody, an almost reverential hush fell over the audience, which then began to sway as one.

At that point, John Henry walked toward the side of the stage where Henrietta stood, unsuspecting, and coaxed her out to the middle of the stage.

She did not go easily, but she went. Pointing to the microphone, John Henry said, "Sing."

"I can't," she protested.

But sing she did, and with all the passion of a pent-up heart – just as the great lady of soul had done on the recording that launched her to national fame. In the audience, many a girl and boy, man and woman too, mouthed the lyrics as Henrietta sang the opening words of this sizzling love song: *"If you want my lovin'. . ."*

Recovering quickly from a somewhat tentative start, Henrietta soon found the song's groove and settled in to ride it for all she was worth. And when Marcella, Barbara, and Angela moved in behind her to sing backup, they soon had the crowd singing aloud with them. It was one of the highest of highlights in an evening of highlights.

Henrietta and the girls took several bows to enthusiastic applause, and then, to the surprise of Billy, John Henry and the whole band, Henrietta announced that the next number "by Billy and the Classics," would be one of her favorites, by the Hollies. She added, "Anybody who don't like this next number need to contact the coroner." Handing the microphone to John Henry, she exited stage left beaming with satisfaction.

Billy looked in surprise at John Henry; John Henry looked in surprise at Billy and shrugged his shoulders; and then Billy approached the microphone and began playing what was still another famous introduction, this one featuring guitar notes alternating with crashing drum beats.

John Henry hurried to the microphone and announced: "And now, ladies and gentlemen, here's 'Long Cool Woman In a Black Dress.'" Then, remembering Henrietta's christening of the band, he added: "by Billy Randolph and the Classics."

But Billy had sung only the first few words, "Saturday night I was downtown. . .," when a clamor went up from the crowd. Seemingly from out of nowhere, a man had scrambled onto the stage at one end, shoved Henrieta to the floor when she tried to stop him, and then stormed across the stage, shouting, "STOP! STOP! STOP THIS TRAVESTY!" Racing past Billy, who was at stage center, the man charged toward John Henry and began flailing at his face. "Stop this barbaric music!" he screamed.

"Mr. Montrose!" Henrietta cried.

"Mr. Montrose!" Billy yelled.

"Stop that SOB," somebody in the audience shouted. Squeals and screams pierced the night as the audience at first recoiled from the fracas, and then rushed forward again the better to see it.

As John Henry struggled to escape the clutches of Mr. Montrose, who now was trying to wrestle him to the stage floor, Billy, his guitar still slung around his neck, lunged to restrain Mr. Montrose, who was screaming over and over, "You black sonofabitch, you've interfered with me for the last time!"

Next, Mr. Montrose turned on Billy, swinging at him wildly with his fists and striking him in the face. Seeing Billy under attack, Dash, who had rushed over first to see about Henrietta, then sprinted across the stage in split seconds to cold-cock Mr. Montrose with a violin he had grabbed from Barbara to use as a weapon. With a mighty swing, he busted the violin over Mr. Montrose's head, and sent him sprawling into the audience and to the ground. "Take that, you cracker!" Dash yelled. "Take that!"

Encircled by some members of the audience, Mr. Montrose was helped to his feet by two or three men who advised him to leave. "Mister, you better get out of here while you still can," one of them told him. "The cops are coming."

Dusting himself off, Mr. Montrose walked away shouting imprecations too nasty to record here, and with his departure the crowd closed ranks again in front of the stage, looking to see if the people onstage were all right and hoping the show would now resume. But on stage, Billy, John Henry, Henrietta, Rich, Barbara, Marcella, Clifford, Angela, and Sonny were staring in amazement at Dash, who, still angry, was shaking his fist and staring daggers at the retreating back of Mr. Montrose.

Henrietta said it first: "Dash! You can talk!"

Billy stared at Dash in wonder. "Sonofagun, Dash!"

"Amazing," said the other band members.

"*Great godamighty*," John Henry exclaimed. "A miracle!"

"Two miracles," Henrietta exclaimed. "You didn't limp when you went after old man Montrose! You ran like a deer." Still amazed, Henrietta added, "Come here, boy, let me look at you."

In front of Henrietta and the others, Dash walked a few steps back and forth as if to see for himself that he could walk without limping. Finding that indeed he could, he flashed a big grin and shouted, "Hallelujah!" Now amazed himself, he stared at Henrietta, who stared back at him until they both rushed toward each other to embrace.

The excitement over, John Henry looked at Billy's face and then brought him to Henrietta so she could examine it, too.

"Busted lip is all," she said. Pulling a lady's handkerchief from her pocket, she pressed it to the wound. "How do you feel?"

"OK," Billy mumbled through sore lips, "but ah don fink ah kin sing ennymo tonite."

"Can you play?" Dash asked.

Billy held his hand up and examined it and then took a visual inventory of himself, and said, "Yes."

"Somebody hand me my guitar," Dash said to the band members. When he had the bass guitar in hand, he said, "C'mon, Billy. We've got a song to finish. You play lead guitar and this time *I'll* sing."

Seconds later, Dash's new-found voice soared into the night, and the rest of the band soared with him in paying tribute one more time to *"a long cool woman in a black dress, just a five-nine beautiful tall. . ."*

The number ended to spirited applause, and perhaps the most spirited came from Mrs. Randolph, who had arrived unnoticed by those who knew her and was now making her way to stage center to give Dash a big hug.

At that, John Henry announced an intermission and encouraged the audience to "come back in 20 minutes and we'll crank up some more of that old-time rock 'n' roll for you."

They huddled onstage and talked as the crowd drifted away. They had so much to talk about that they all tried to talk at once — Mr. Montrose's attack, Dash's miraculous recovery, the crowd's reception of their music. But after a while Mrs. Randolph quieted them with a raised hand.

"First, news about your father, Billy."

Everybody fell silent.

Mrs. Randolph smiled. To Billy, she announced, "The doctors say your father will make a full recovery — but he will be convalescing, at home, for a long time."

"That's great news!" Billy said. "Thank the lord."

All the others nodded their agreement.

"But what about the radio station?" Rich asked. "Every time I come to your house, Mr. Randolph is at work."

"Mr. Randolph's work habits are changed as of now," Mrs. Randolph said.

"But who'll run the station?" Billy asked. "You can't leave that to Mr. Montrose. He—"

Mrs. Randolph held up her hand again. "I saw everything, Billy. I was watching – in amazement, I confess – when to my further amazement Mr. Montrose ran onto the stage and started fighting. I saw–" she looked directly at John Henry, and Henrietta, and then at Barbara "—and heard it all. Whether or not he knows it yet, Mr. Montrose is no longer employed by WSOF."

Billy repeated himself. "But who'll run the radio stations – all of them? You have to have a general manager."

"I'll cross that bridge when I get to it, Billy," his mother said. "Your father has given me his power of attorney, and finding a general manager will be one of the first things on my list come morning. But for now I'm tired. It's been a long, long day. I'm going home."

"I'll go with you," Henrietta said, moving to her side.

"Don't let them stay out too late, Mr. Jones," Billy's mother said.

The two women began to leave arm-in-arm.

Shaking his head, Billy approached John Henry. "What a night! Wonder what can happen next?"

Watching Henrietta and Mrs. Randolph leave the stage, John Henry saw them stop to speak to a stranger, a man, and point back to the group on stage before moving on. John Henry did not know the man, but he recognized him as one of the event's judges.

John Henry smiled and put his arm around Billy's shoulder. "I suspect, Billy-boy, that you're about to find out."

Seconds later, the strange man came onto the stage and stopped to speak to some of the musicians, who then followed him as he approached Billy and John Henry. In a slightly formal manner, he addressed Billy.

"Young man, it is my great pleasure to tell you that you and your group have been declared the winner of this year's competition. You and your band will shortly receive a certificate to that effect – and a trophy duly inscribed.. Congratulations."

A cheer went up from the other musicians, but Billy was not only too stunned by the news to join in, he was worried about what his father would think and say. The band had, after all, represented Radio Station WSOF. Wouldn't people laugh at such a turn of events? He flashed a worried look at John Henry. Would John Henry get the blame for all this?

"I know what you're thinking, Billy-boy, but I'm sure that your dad will find out sooner or later that his son is a chip off the ol' block."

Chapter Nine

Time: One Month Later

WHEN BILLY heard again the sound that had awakened him, he sat up in bed and listened intently. Someone nearby was crying. It had to be his mother; no one else was there. He looked at the clock by his bed. It was after one o'clock in the morning!

Easing barefoot out of his room, he first checked his mother's bedroom. It was empty, the bed still made. But now he heard a stirring downstairs.

Descending the carpeted stairs, he saw that the door to the library was ajar. Soft light leaked from the doorway into the hallway, and Billy realized then that his mother must have been working late, just as his father had so often done. Going closer, he saw his mother, still wearing her work clothes, seated at his father's desk and staring at some papers spread out before her. She was no longer crying, but the light from the lamp illumined tear-stained cheeks.

Pushing the door open wider, he entered. "Mother, what's wrong?"

Surprised, Mrs. Randolph sat up straight and wiped her eyes. "Billy! What are you doing up at this hour? Go back to bed."

"I heard you crying. It woke me up. Mother, what's wrong?"

"Nothing," she said. "I'm worried about your father."

"But I thought—"

"So did the doctors, but this evening he took a turn for the worse." Sge breathed deeply, raggedly. "Now they say he needs a heart transplant or. . ."

135

"Or what?"

"Or he'll be dead within six months."

Billy was shaken. "Can't they do it – get him a new heart, I mean?"

"There's a waiting list. He's on it."

Billy was relieved. Somehow things would work out. "Well, then. . ."

"You don't just wait your turn; you also wait for a good match."

"Even so. . ."

"Your father has AB negative blood, the rarest type."

Billy braced himself: "How rare?"

Mrs. Randolph began to cry again. 'They say only 0.6 percent of the human population has that blood type."

Her words struck Billy almost as a physical blow, but he struggled to hide their effect from his mother.

After wiping her eye, Mrs. Randolph gave Billy a sorrowful look and said, "But that's not all." She took a deep, ragged breath. "I guess you might as well know now as later. We're about to lose WSOF."

He started to speak, but she raised a hand to stop him.

"I'm just not the businessman your father is. I've done everything I can think of to cut operating expenses, but we're still losing money. Market *and* money. We're losing market share. And when market share drops, advertising revenue drops. Simple as that." She heaved a sigh. "Believe me, I've tried everything to reverse the downward trend."

"Not everything," Billy said. He spoke softly but with the candor of youth.

His mother was taken aback by his comment. "What do you mean?"

"You haven't tried changing formats."

His mother gasped. "That's simply unthinkable, Billy."

He looked into her tear-stained face. "'You can't solve a problem with the same kind of thinking that caused it.'"

She looked amazed, confused. "What?"

He shrugged. "Learned it in school. Einstein, I think. But it's true."

She scoffed. "Albert Einstein didn't run radio stations."

He remained composed and spoke softly again. "Mother, the music on WSOF is no better than elevator music. It's awful and it's out of tune with the times. It isn't even good soft music. It's music for people who. . . who don't really like music."

She gave her son a pitying look. "It's late, Billy. Go on back to bed."

"But, Mother—"

She cut him off. "I'm going to bed, myself. It's been a long week. Now get some rest." She began gathering into a stack the papers spread across the desk and somehow knocked a ring of keys to the floor.

Billy picked up the keys, recognizing them as the keys to the station. He held them out to her.

"Just put them in the desk drawer," she said while turning off the desk lamp. "That long drawer in the center. I won't need them again until I get back from New York."

"New York?"

"I leave on Sunday, day after tomorrow. Be back next weekend." She sighed. "Yes. One more plea to the banks for an extension on our loans. They've told me not to bother to come, but I have to try, at least."

"Have a safe flight. And good luck."

Billy slid open the drawer, put the keys inside, gave his mother a good-night (and consoling) kiss on the cheek, and then went back to his room and to bed – but not back to sleep for a long time. Over and over in his mind, he turned an idea, examining it first one way and then another, a plan to save WSOF. Full of resolve, he eventually slept.

Chapter Ten

Time: Next Day

JOHN HENRY recoiled at the very idea. "Oh, no, Billy-boy, I can't do that! Sorry. Where did you get such an idea?"

Billy writhed in frustration. "But, John Henry, Dash and I can't do this without your help. You've been a deejay – Henrietta told me that. And you've got all those great old records. And you can drive. How can we get there if you won't take us?"

Billy had gone looking for John Henry and found him in the garage, where he was cleaning the carburetor of a lawn mower. John Henry looked hard at Billy. "Son, you can't just break into a radio station and take it over."

142

Billy writhed some more. "But you won't be breaking in—"

"You right about that, 'cause *I* won't be there."

"I have the key to the station." Billy reached into the pocket of his jeans and withdrew his mother's key-ring. "And the station belongs to my father. We *won't* be breaking in; we'll only be *walking* in."

"To take over the place," John Henry reminded him.

"To *save* it," Billy insisted.

John Henry looked toward the house. "Where's your mother?"

"Beauty parlor. Getting ready for her trip to New York, I guess."

"Where's Henrietta?"

"Went with her. Dash, too. Mom's dropping them off at the speech therapist's."

"That's going to be one surprised speech therapist, ain't it?" John Henry turned the carburetor filter this way and that, making sure it was clean. After a moment, he spoke again. "I'm sure you and Dash got Henrietta's permission for him to help you to do all this." He gave Billy a dubious look.

Billy didn't say anything. He knew that John Henry knew better. Henrietta would not in a thousand years give her approval for such a venture.

John Henry went on: "You still haven't told me where you got such an idea."

Billy told him about the talk he'd had with his mother the night before, how he'd found her crying in the library, how she said they were about to lose the station because it wasn't making money, how he'd suggested changing the station's format, and what she had said about that idea. He even repeated his quote from Einstein.

John Henry thought it over. "Sounds like you've done all you can do, Billy."

"No, John Henry. Doing nothing about a problem is never the solution."

"Who says?"

"Well, Stevie Wonder, for one." Billy broke into song: *"'Cause if you really want to hear our views, you haven't done nothing.'"*

John Henry was taken aback, but amused, too. "Title song from the album, 1974. Did you know that the Jackson Five sang backup on that tune?"

Billy smiled. "I do now."

"Did you know Stevie Wonder was singing about civil rights."

"Do now."

"Well, tell me, schoolboy: Did you know that the title echoed a famous statement by a political philosopher named Edmund Burke?"

This had become a game. Billy humored John Henry. "Which was?"

"'All that is necessary for evil to triumph is for good men to do nothing.'"

Billy's face brightened. With self-conscious guile, he said, "*You're* a good man, John Henry. Will you do nothing to help save WSOF?"

Ouch, thought John Henry. But he said, "I agree the format needs changing, Billy. Needs it bad. But I'm not looking to spend the rest of my life behind bars. Sorry."

"Then I'll just have to find a way to do it myself," said Billy, turning to leave.

John Henry reached out and put a hand on Billy's shoulder. "Wait a minute, boy. What you about to do?"

Billy turned back. "*I'll* drive me and Dash to the station. I know the way and I know where the key to Dad's car is, and I have my learner's permit."

"You need a licensed adult in the car to drive with a learner's permit."

"Not if I don't get caught."

"What will you use for music? All the records are mine."

"Remember those you loaned us? I put 'em on tape. Want to lend me some more?"

Now it was John Henry's turn to writhe in frustration. "Billy," he said, "you boys can't do this by yourself. You just can't."

"That's why I came to you."

John Henry sighed. "Okay, just for the sake of argument, tell me your plan."

Billy explained: The station signed on at six every morning. He had gone there with his dad many times to open up for the day and he knew how easy it was to sign onto the air. It was as easy as, well, throwing a switch. And he knew which switch to throw. Moreover, he had also sat many times with the DJs and seen how to introduce and spin records. They had even let him cue up and introduce records, and then send them out over the air. Piece of cake. "I will get there early enough to be the first one there.

147

Then I'll lock the door behind us so nobody else can get in. I'll sign on at six o'clock and announce that WSOF has changed formats. Then Dash and I will play rock 'n' roll music until. . ."

"Until what?" John Henry demanded.

Billy shrugged and admitted that he hadn't gotten farther than that in his planning.

"Billy, you and Dash can't do this by yourselves. I told you that." John Henry's look and tone of voice were severe.

Billy sighed. "My father is in the hospital in intensive care, and in trying to fill his shoes my poor mother is just in over her head. That leaves it to me to come up with something." Billy began to walk away.

John Henry called after him. "You're asking for trouble. And you'll get Dash in trouble, too."

Billy walked on, saying nothing.

Chapter Eleven

Time: Early Monday Morning

THE NIGHT was clear, the moon was bright, and the first light of dawn shimmered on the eastern horizon when Billy and Dash sneaked out of the house, crept across the yard, opened the front doors of Mr. Randolph's Lincoln Continental, and eased in. Once they were in, Billy slid the key into the ignition, looked at Dash with apprehension, and then turned the key. Both boys sagged a bit in relief when the car's engine started smoothly and purred quietly in idle. Leaving the headlights off, Billy put the car in reverse and eased out of the garage into the driveway. Poised there, both boys looked fixedly at the house, half expecting a light to come on inside, for Henrietta slept in the big house when both of Billy's parents were away from home. But the house remained still and dark.

Billy was about to put the gear into "drive," when his door popped open and he heard a man say, "Move over, Billy-boy. I'll drive."

Billy nearly squealed, first in fright, and then in delight. "John Henry! You scared the life out of me."

"Me, too!" said Dash, grinning from ear to ear.

Tossing a gym bag onto the back seat, John Henry settled under the steering wheel, put the car into gear, and rolled to the street, where he took a left turn and headed toward Peachtree Street, three blocks away. "Sorry I startled you, but I saw that you two were determined to go through with this fool plan, and I just couldn't let you go it alone."

Both boys thanked him effusively for coming with them. They felt *greatly* relieved to have John Henry with them.

"I don't need thanks," John Henry groused; "what I need is my head examined." After a moment, he said. "Station's on Peachtree, isn't it?"

"Fifteen hundred," Billy said.

At Peachtree, John Henry turned right and headed toward downtown Atlanta. "Not too late to turn back," he sang out in a taunting voice.

Billy and Dash exchanged looks. As one, they said, "Keep going."

Daylight was approaching when they reached the three-story building housing the radio station. John Henry pulled into Mr. Randolph's reserved parking space, near the recessed front entrance. Billy and Dash got out, each carrying a satchel that normally held school books, and marched to the station's front entrance.

John Henry was right behind them. "Still not too late," he sang out.

The boys marched on in silence.

At the station's big double doors, Billy held out his hand to John Henry. "The door key is on the key ring you've got, John Henry." John Henry handed over the keys, and seconds later the big plate-glass doors of WSOF swung open. Billy pointed toward a wall. "Get the lights, Dash, please." Seconds later the hallways and some offices were ablaze with light. "This way," said Billy.

"Don't forget the door!" Dash called.

"Oops!" Billy turned back and re-locked the door. Then he stepped aside while Dash pulled a chain from his satchel, weaved it around the handles of the big doors, and then cinched the two ends with a bicycle lock. Now

153

no one could open the doors from the outside. He pushed on them to make sure.

"Good work," said Billy.

"Now the sign," Dash said.

From his satchel, Billy pulled out a rolled, hand-lettered sign that read "UNDER NEW MANAGEMENT. OFF LIMITS TILL FURTHER NOTICE." He positioned the sign head-high on one of the doors and held it there while Dash, extracting a dispenser of clear tape from one of his pockets, affixed the sign to the glass by its four corners. Anybody approaching the doors could read it.

In spite of himself, John Henry was impressed. Obviously the boys had planned this mission well.

Billy and Dash examined their handiwork and exchanged high fives before moving on into the building. At the intersection of two long hallways, Billy asked Dash to "check the back door." He held up a key. "I think this is the only key to the back, but we need to know that the door wasn't left unlocked."

Dash said, "Check," and moved down a hall that led toward the back of the building.

Billy turned to John Henry. "The studio's this way," He walked down another hallway to a door over which a darkened light fixture said "ON THE AIR." It was then that Billy noticed for the first time that John Henry was carrying a backpack. He pointed. "What's that?"

John Henry blushed. "You asked to borrow some records." He held the backpack aloft. "Well, here they are."

Billy nearly danced with glee. "Oh, man, thank you, John Henry. Thank you, thank you!"

John Henry gave Billy a solemn look. "So don't say again that I haven't done nothing."

Billy beamed and said, "Deal!" Then he and John Henry went through the door to the studio, turning on the room lights. Right behind them came Dash, flashing a thumbs-up to Billy: the back door was secured.

The production studio featured a wall of glass that overlooked Peachtree Street. The window had been one of Mr. Randolph's better ideas. Passersby on foot often stopped to watch announcers at work and sometimes to wave a greeting. Announcers liked the big window because they could see outdoors when working long hours at a stretch. They also could see what the weather outside was like instead of merely read about it, and a glance at Peachtree Street gave them a good idea of downtown traffic conditions in the city. But at closing each day the blinds were drawn, and this morning, stealth being the order of the day, they remained drawn.

Inside, the main feature of the production studio, which was soundproof, was a U-shaped table or desk at which the announcer or announcers sat at microphones that were suspended above an audio console. Close at hand were a soundboard, a computer screen and keyboard, and a telephone console that appeared elaborate enough to serve as a small switchboard. Aside from a few more chairs scattered about, for interviewees or guests, the room held no other furniture.

"Things have changed a bit since I worked radio," John Henry said, looking around the room. He could see that WSOF's production set-up was basically a one-man operation. The audio console especially interested him. It could be manipulated by a lone announcer. In his day, it had taken at least two people to get a show on the air: an announcer and an engineer, who usually sat in an adjacent room or booth with a window that overlooked the studio.

Billy began rummaging in his satchel. "What time is it?" he asked.

"Twenty to six," Dash pointed to a clock on the wall.

"What time do the morning people come in?" John Henry asked.

"Some, any minute now," Billy said.

Dash headed for the door. "I'll check out the front," he said.

Billy put his satchel on the table, near the deejay's seat. Next he pulled one of the other chairs closer and invited John Henry to join him near the microphones. "What should we open with?" Billy asked. "After the announcement, I mean."

"Been thinkin' about that," said John Henry. "Gotta be Chuck Berry's 'Roll Over Beethoven.' It's not one of my favorites, but if there's a national anthem of rock 'n' roll, that's it. He opened his backpack. "Got it right here."

Billy nodded and smiled, and John Henry placed the little 45 record on a turntable and cued it. "Ready," he told Billy.

Dash re-entered the studio and joined them in the slot of the U-shaped desk. "Guy standing out front wondering what's going on," he reported. "I didn't let him see me."

"Probably Tom Hotchkiss," Billy said. "He usually works the early-morning show."

"What do you think he'll do?" said Dash.

Billy laughed. "Start looking for another job – unless he likes rock 'n' roll."

John Henry pointed to the clock. "Almost time."

Billy pulled a notebook from his satchel, laid it where he could read from it, and settled into the deejay's chair, his hand on the master switch.

Dash stared at the clock and counted down the seconds: "10, 9, 8, 7, 6, 5, 4. . ."

At six o'clock on the dot, Billy toggled a switch on the big console in front of him, and the sign over the studio door lit up. WSOF was now on the air. Pushing another switch, Billy leaned toward the mike and said calmly, "Good morning, Atlanta. This is your host Billy Randolph with an important announcement. As of this moment WSOF is no longer a soft-music station. It is now a rock 'n' roll station."

Dash raised his fists in a victorious salute and Billy raised his in response. John Henry just smiled and shook his head.

Billy continued: "My companions and I have taken control of the station, and until further notice it is on lockdown. WSOF employees may take the day off." He paused. "Allow me to explain: As the son of the owner, John Richard Randolph, I accept full responsibility for the takeover. I didn't have my parents' permission to do this or to change the format, and I know that my father, if able to protest, would not approve of this format change. But desperate circumstances call for desperate measures. WSOF is in financial trouble; my father is in the hospital, incapacitated; and my poor mother Gloria, though a wonderful woman and mother, is feeling simply overwhelmed."

Dash and John Henry nodded solemn agreement.

Billy continued. "She is, in fact, in New York City right now to seek, again, financial help from bankers. But I say we don't need a loan; what we need is a change of format, and this is it!"

Then, affecting a radio voice so professional-sounding that it surprised John Henry and delighted Dash, Billy read from the proclamation that he and Dash had written. "Now on with the revolution! The new format of this station is actually no format. We're simply going to play the best of the music you grew up with – Ray Charles, Aretha Franklin, Elvis, James Brown, the Beatles, Marvin Gaye. The list could, and will, go on and on: the Eagles, Creedence Clearwater, Carol King, Maria Cary, Billy Joel, the Rolling Stones, Elton John, Stevie Wonder – in other words, the best that popular music has produced – and is still producing." Billy glanced at John Henry, who nodded; he was ready with the record – but he was not ready at all for what Billy did next. To a waking Atlanta, Billy announced, "And now here's my co-host, John Henry Jones, to get WSOF off on the right foot in its new musical direction."

Taken aback, a flustered John Henry waved both hands and his head to say no, no, no, but in a split second his professional instincts took over. He leaned toward his microphone and said, "Got just the thing here, Billy-boy: I call it the national anthem of rock 'n' roll, Chuck Berry's 'Roll Over Beethoven,'" He then pushed a switch on the turntable, and the first strains of Berry's classic call to a musical revolution, sounded way back in 1956, blasted over the air to some very surprised faithful WSOF listeners out in radio-land. At the downbeat, Billy and John Henry high-fived each other, and Dash was enjoying the moment so much that he nearly collapsed in mirth.

Almost immediately, lights on the telephone console began to light up – first one, then two, then three and four. Billy and Dash had anticipated phone calls, unwelcome ones anyhow, and had resolved not to answer for at least the first hour.

John Henry, who would not have answered the phone anyhow, was busy sorting through his backpack for more records. Nevertheless, he dead-panned: "If it's the police, I'm not in."

Dash laughed. "If it's Henrietta, I ran away to join the Navy."

163

Meantime, Chuck Berry was proclaiming: "...*I got the rocking pneumonia; I need a shot of rhythm and blues. . .*" And moments later, John Henry's voice rode in over the last strains of Berry's classic call to musical arms: "We hear you, Chuck, baby. We *all* could use a shot of rhythm and blues. So get outta that bed, Atlanta, and wash yo' face and hands. It's a new day in the Big A, and a brand new WSOF is gonna 'roll like a wheel in a Georgia cotton field to 'Honey, Hush,' by Big Joe Turner, the Boss of the Blues. When this one first came out, rock 'n' roll was so young it was still called rhythm 'n' blues." Then, riding on a red-hot piano intro, Big Joe's deep bass voice came up right under John Henry's patter, and when John Henry ramped up the volume the song seemed to take off at a gallop *"Come in this house, stop that yakety-yak. . ."*

Billy smiled. This music was so much more to his liking than what he was accustomed to hear on WSOF. Soft music was all right in its place, but for all-day listening it was, well, *too* soft. Too other-worldly. Too not-with-it. Even when it had rhythm, it lacked a pulse. Rock 'n' roll was here and now. Alive!

He smiled even more broadly when John Henry introduced the next recording, one of his and Dash's favorites: "Memphis Soul Stew," by King Curtis. John Henry said, "If this one doesn't wake you up, you're ready for the coroner, so go on back to sleep and rest in peace."

Billy loved the way this record began, with a sustained introduction in which Curtis recites the "recipe" for Memphis Soul Stew to introduce the band's musicians, including himself on that scalding saxophone of his: "Gimme a half a teacup of bass," "a pound of fatback drums," "four tablespoons of boiling Memphis guitar," "a little pinch of organ," "a half pint of horn," and then "bring to a boil," at which point the band, all playing together now, blasts off as if streaking into musical orbit.

Yes, sir, Billy told himself, *it was a good day when John Henry Jones came to work for the Randolphs.* The man could do anything! Sing, dance – though he hadn't done either in a long time. Hadn't been a deejay, either, in years and years, but his patter and delivery were lively and smooth, and his taste in music was, well, unbeatable.

In fact, as John Henry spun one great record after another in the station's first hour as a new stop on Atlanta's radio dial, Billy had the feeling that the city was getting more than a new WSOF, it was also getting a new radio personality, too. The man was a font of musical knowledge and seemed to know interesting things about every record he played, information that made a record more than, well, just another record. It helped you *understand* the music, helped you understand the origins of rock 'n' roll, helped you fit the music into the soundtrack of your own life, and all without talking too much or sounding, well, tutorial. Why, in this first hour alone, he had tossed off gems that anybody who really loved music would appreciate:

-- "Roll Over Beethoven" was No. 97 on *Rolling Stone* magazine's list of the 500 Greatest Songs of All Times.

--Another of Berry's recordings, "Johnny B. Goode," had inspired countless teenage boys to take up the electric guitar and become rock 'n' roll musicians themselves.

--Big Joe Turner, one of the earliest of rock 'n' rollers, was born Joseph Vernon Turner Jr., in Kansas City in 1911. Began as a youth singing on the city's street corners.

"Some historians," John Henry told listeners, "credit Turner's version of 'Shake, Rattle and Roll' with launching the rock 'n' roll era. It didn't; there were earlier records. But it certainly didn't hurt the movement. Released in the spring of 1954, months before the version by Bill Haley and the Comets, Big Joe's record hit the top of the R&B charts in June of that year. It ranks Number 126 among the greatest of all time."

Even John Henry's trivia was interesting, Billy noted with admiration. Both "Memphis Soul Stew" and "Chain of Fools" were produced in 1967, John Henry said, "a vintage year in a vintage decade of great rock 'n' roll recordings." And "Chain of Fools" was written by Don Covay, a singer who racked up hits of his own, among them "See-Saw," a catchy tune from 1966 featuring what John Henry called "some of the strangest backup singing ever." Pausing a beat, he then declared, "But if you can hear this song without starting to shimmy and shake, see a doctor – soon!"

With that, he played "See-Saw," and sure enough, Billy, hearing it for the first time, found it exactly as described: a bit strange, but so rhythmic, with its funky piano, subtle bass, staccato brass, and bouncy beat that you could not stay still while listening to it: *". . . Your love is like a see-saw, up, down, all around, like a see-saw."* In fact, before he knew it, Billy was on his feet, swaying to the music, and he didn't sit again, *couldn't* sit, for a solid hour as John Henry played (and commented on) one terrific song after another, ranging from soul to blues to funk to jazz. Among them:

--"Mr. Pitiful," by Otis Redding: "As good today as it was in 1964 when first released."

--"Gotta Get It Worked On," by Delbert McClinton: "If you, too, need to get it worked on, this tune will do the trick, guaranteed."

--"Honky Cat," by Elton John: "Elton John is a musical genius; it's that simple."

--"I'm Walkin'," by Fats Domino: "The man had 37 Top 40 singles! That says it all."

169

--"Eleanor Rigby," by the Beatles: "A musical landmark: with this number, rock 'n' roll came of age."

--"Eleanor Rigby," by the Jazz Crusaders. "And this version, with its great piano exploration by Joe Sample, is further proof of just how good this song was – and still is."

--"Will You Still Love Me Tomorrow?" by the Shirelles: "Voted Best Song of 1960 and, thanks to this marvelous girls' group, ranked as the 110th greatest song of all time."

--"Searchin'," by the Coasters: "Even my mother-in-law liked this song."

--"Mojo" by Jimmy Smith: "Who said nobody could make a Hammond organ swing?"

--"Swanee River Rock," by Ray Charles: "Stephen Foster, meet Mr. Tchaikovsky."

--"Steamroller Blues," James Taylor: "He did a lot of versions of this song, the older he got, the better he did it. Draw your own conclusions."

--"You're the Best Thing That Ever Happened To Me," by Gladys Knight: "There's no better female singer than this lady anywhere. In fact, her only equal is Barbra Streisand."

--"Long Cool Woman in a Black Dress," the Hollies. "The quintessential rock 'n' roll number. If you don't like this record, you just don't like rock 'n' roll."

--"You Better Leave My Little Girl Alone," by Stevie Ray Vaughan: "The man could make a guitar talk."

As John Henry was introducing the next record, the hour hand of the big clock on the wall slipped past eight. He signaled to Dash and John Henry that he was going to take a look out front.

Caught up in the music, which was piped through speakers located throughout the building, Billy pulled up short as he approached

171

the front and saw people, a crowd of people, gathered outside. Hotchkiss was still out there, and Billy also recognized Clarence Bigham and Susan Thrift, WSOF salespeople; Sam Wells, a station custodian; and Helen Truesdale, the receptionist, a young woman in her twenties. But who were those other people? Most seemed to be milling around near the entrance, talking to each other and not watching the door, but Miss Truesdale spotted Billy and motioned excitedly for him to come open the door. Billy went to the door and smiled at her, but he pointed to the sign on the door and gave a shrug of helplessness.

Signaling for him to wait, Miss Truesdale alerted some of the others to his presence. She then fished an envelope from her purse, and somebody handed her a pen. She scrawled something on the back of the envelope, and then held it to the door for Billy to read. It said: WE ARE ON YOUR SIDE. LET US IN TO HELP!

Though surprised, Billy quickly weighed the appeal. They *could* use some help; that was for sure. It was one thing to hijack the station; it was another to make the *coup* a successful one. Signaling for Miss Truesdale to wait, he hurried back to the studio to confer with Dash and John Henry. When he re-entered, Dash was pointing frantically to the telephone console; the buttons for all the lines, at least twenty of them, were still blinking. John Henry was introducing "Mockingbird," by James Taylor and Carly Simon, and when the record began playing, Billy told them about Helen Truesdale's offer — and was surprised at how eager both of them were to accept it.

"I see it as a good sign," said John Henry. He laughed. "It could have been 'Come out with your hands up!' In any case, we do need help. There aren't enough of us to keep going here all day. I didn't get my beauty rest last night and I'm tired already."

173

Dash pointed. "And look at that phone console all lit up. Been that way since 6:05. What if the callers are prospective customers?"

"Then that settles it," Billy said. "Dash, let's go let the employees in. John Henry, I'll get you some relief soon as I can."

John Henry waved to them and the two boys started toward the front entrance.

Chapter Twelve

DASH REMOVED the chain from the doors, and Billy opened them just widely enough for Miss Truesdale and the other station employees to squeeze through one at a time. It was no easy task to get in, for the crowd outside had grown larger and people pushed toward the doors when they saw them about to be opened.

First to be let in was Miss Truesdale, who pushed through the narrow opening, saying, "Whew! What a crowd out there!"

Right behind her came Susan Thrift and Clarence Bigham, WSOF salespeople, Sam Wells, custodian, and Hotchkiss, the previously exiled DJ.

Nodding toward the throng of people outside, Billy asked, "Who are all those people? Why are they here?"

All the employees tried to speak at once: "Reporters! Fans! Spectators."

"Reporters?" Billy was puzzled.

"You and your companions are the talk of the town," said Hotchkiss. "I'll bet every news outfit in Atlanta has reporters out there."

Wow! Billy thought

"And there's an even larger crowd at the big studio window," said Miss Thrift. "They probably want to get a look at your new DJ. He's terrific!"

"Big window?" Now Dash looked puzzled. He hadn't noticed the blinds.

"You guys are all over the news this morning," Bigham told them. "Your takeover of WSOF has been on all the TV and radio news shows in the city."

"You've pulled off a brilliant publicity stunt," Hotchkiss said.

"Hear! Hear!" the others shouted.

Billy and Dash looked at each other, bewildered, but then, awareness dawning, they broke into wide smiles. "We are? We did?"

Bigham, the station's sales manager, smiled broadly, too. "And the advertisers came running!" he said. "Why, I had signed more than $20,000 in new advertising before eight a.m. My phone started ringing at 6:05 this morning."

"I've signed that much new business, too," said Miss Thrift. "And the morning is still young!" She laughed with delight.

Holy cow! Billy thought. Maybe the station could be saved, after all. He and Dash exchanged looks of amazement.

Suddenly all business, Billy turned to the station's custodian. "Mr. Wells, please go open the blinds. Tell John Henry I said it was okay."

178

Wells hurried away down the hall, saying, "I want to meet him anyhow. He's good!"

Turning next to Miss Truesdale, Billy said, "People have been trying to call in all morning, but we wouldn't answer the phone. Please begin handling the calls. If it's a new advertiser, turn them over to Mr. Bigham or Miss Thrift. If it's an old advertiser who wants his money back, tell him we'll send it."

Miss Truesdale hurried to her desk, near the front entrance, and began taking calls.

To Hotchkiss, Billy said, "Can you relieve John Henry at the top of the hour? He needs a break."

"You bet!" He checked his watch. It was 8:50.

"Ask to use his records,' Billy said. "And before you leave work today, trash the station's soft-music library."

Hotchkiss beamed. "Glad to!"

179

Then, looking around for guidance, Billy asked, "What about the people outside?"

"Just tell 'em show's over," Bigham offered. "We've all got to get to work."

Billy said, "Come on, Dash. We'll both tell 'em."

But when they stepped outside, the crowd surged around them and, as with a mind of its own, swept them toward Peachtree Street, where they were accosted at the sidewalk by reporters who shoved microphones at them from every direction and, all speaking at once, shouted questions from all sides.

"Whose idea was this!" called a young woman holding a microphone bearing the call letters of WSB, Atlanta's venerable radio (and television) station.

Awed for a moment, Billy merely raised his hand. Up and down Peachtree Street, he saw cars double-parked, many of them bearing the logos of Atlanta radio and TV stations. And there must have been a thousand people thronged at WSOF's big studio window, he guessed, amazed. Slowly his attention returned to the shouted questions from the crowd.

"Who's that terrific DJ you've got and where did you find him?" cried a young man who identified himself as a reporter for WYAW, an all-news station.

"Aren't you members of the band that won the Atlanta Arts Festival?" This question was fired at them by a young woman who was accompanied by a WXIA-TV cameraman.

"How's your father? What's the latest on his condition?" called someone, evidently a man, from somewhere behind Billy and Dash.

But before the boys could answer came a question that brought a big laugh from the crowd, "Do your mothers know where you boys are?" And this was followed by an answer that brought an even bigger laugh: "They certainly do – and here *we* are!"

181

Pushing through the crowd toward Billy and Dash were Mrs. Randolph and Henrietta — and neither one looked happy.

"Mom!" said Billy, stunned. She was supposed to be in New York!

"Grandma!" cried Dash, scared *and* stunned.

"You his mother?" someone called to Henrietta as she brushed past him.

"Only one he's ever had," Henrietta said in a huff, "but I'm close to disowning him."

In the center of the throng, Mrs. Randolph, a stern look on her face that Billy knew all too well, stepped in front of Billy and Dash and announced, "I am the co-owner of WSOF and the acting general manager. Please direct your questions to me."

Billy leaned forward and whispered to his mother, "I can explain, Mom. Please don't un-do what we've done this morning."

She whispered back, scolding, "We didn't get the loan, Billy, and now we might not even be able to sell the station. What in the world were you thinking?"

He set in to explain, but his mother either ignored him or simply didn't hear him, perhaps because Mr. Bigham had pushed urgently through the crowd right behind her and Henrietta, and was now speaking quietly – and earnestly – into her ear. As he talked, Mrs. Randolph's facial features began slowly to morph from stern to surprised to incredibility to a smile, a smile that grew wider and wider, and soon was downright radiant.

Seconds later, Miss Truesdale had shoved her way into the middle of the throng to hand Bigham a steno pad. In turn, Bigham showed Mrs. Randolph some figures written on the pad, figures that made Mrs. Randolph look very, very happy.

Facing the reporters, Mrs. Randolph declaimed, "I'm pleased to announce that WSOF's switch to a new format has been a rousing success and that the station is no longer in danger of failing. I've just been informed that our sales staff has signed more than a quarter of a million dollars in *new* advertising today, and it's not even lunchtime yet."

Someone a few rows back in the crowd yelled: "Was it a publicity stunt? Whose idea was it?"

Mrs. Randolph pulled Billy to her side and put a motherly arm around him. "It was my son's idea," she said, beaming. Pulling Dash to her other side and embracing him, too, she added, "And he and his friend Dash, here, planned the whole thing."

Someone in the crowd yelled, "Is your son your new station manager?"

The crowd laughed. Billy obviously was still a schoolboy.

184

In a congenial tone, Mrs. Randolph said, "That position is open; If you know a suitable candidate, send them our way – now that we'll have a station to manage."

The crowd laughed and applauded, and then Mrs. Randolph added: "And now the press conference, or whatever this was, is over. We have to get back to work."

The crowd applauded again and began to disperse.

As Mrs. Randolph, Henrietta, Dash, and Billy re-entered the building they encountered John Henry, who had been relieved by Hotchkiss of his DJ duties and was now looking for Billy and Dash so he could take them home.

To Billy's surprise, Mrs. Randolph and Henrietta hurried to meet John Henry to thank him heartily for "taking care of Billy and Dash" in their absence. Then Mrs. Randolph asked

John Henry to join her in her husband's office, and led the way there.

Behind the office's big desk, Mrs. Randolph, a small woman, looked smaller still, but she was clearly the authority figure in the room. Addressing John Henry, she said, "I want to reward you for your part in today's, uh, activities. It appears you have talents of which I and my husband were not aware."

John Henry blushed. "Thank you, ma'am. I just didn't want the boys to get in trouble."

"Bless you," Henrietta said. "I'm still gonna skin Dash alive when I get him home, but at least I know now that he was in good hands."

"You have my thanks as a mother, too," Mrs. Randolph said.

For a moment, silence filled the room. But then Mrs. Randolph said, "I'm completely happy with your work as our yardman, John Henry, but it's obvious now that you are

186

capable of very much more." She smiled. "I'm offering you a job as a WSOF DJ. I heard you on the air on my way in from the airport. You were very, very good."

Nobody spoke.

"Will you accept?"

John Henry started to speak, but Billy blurted, "Make him station manager, too!"

When Mrs. Randolph appeared dubious, Billy said, "I was right about the format change, Mom; I'm right about this, too."

Mrs. Randolph appeared to be mulling over what Billy had said. She turned to Henrietta for a second opinion.

Henrietta thought for a moment, "Well, from what I've seen of him, it's a waste of a good man for him to be no more than a yardman. Nothing against yard work, you understand, but Mr. Jones is definitely overqualified for that job -- and probably could do anything he sets his mind to."

Clearly moved, John Henry, said, "Why, thank you, Henrietta. I think a lot of you, too."

"You agree, Dash?" Mrs. Randolph asked.

Dash smiled from ear to ear. "Oh, yeah, a million times yeah. John Henry's the man."

Mrs. Randolph turned next to John Henry. "Well, Mr. Jones?"

He stepped forward to shake her hand. "Meet your new station manager," he said, smiling.

"And DJ," Billy said.

"And DJ," said John Henry.

Henrietta, Dash, and Billy encircled John Henry to congratulate him. They were so engrossed that they barely noticed that Miss Truesdale had entered the room. To Mrs. Randolph, the receptionist said, "You told me not to disturb you, but you'll want to take this call." She went back out, closing the door behind her.

A puzzled look on her face, Mrs. Randolph answered the phone, listened for a few moments, and then began to weep. "Thank God!" she cried. "Oh, thank you, thank you, thank you."

All of them stared at her, waiting.

As she put down the phone, Mrs. Randolph struggled for control of herself and then announced, "That was the hospital calling. A new heart has been found for William. The transplant will take place as soon as possible."

All of them cheered at such good news.

Mrs. Randolph explained: 'Somebody on his way to Grady Memorial Hospital this morning arrived there to find that his grown son had died five minutes before he got to his bedside. He remembered listening to you, Billy, as he dressed for the hospital. His son had the same kind of rare blood as your father's, so your father will be getting his son's heart. Will miracles never cease?"

"Well," Henrietta said, "while we're celebrating, and well we should, let's not forget that our good Samaritan lost his son this morning."

A heartfelt "Amen" arose from all assembled, but, in truth, it did not, could not extinguish the celebratory spirit they all felt.

ACKNOWLEDGEMENTS

(song and performer)

"Mustang Sally," Wilson Pickett

"Spanish Harlem." Ben E. King

"Stubborn Kind of Fellow," Marvin Gaye

"Memphis," Chuck Berry

"Don't Miss That Train," Sister Wynona Carr

"Shotgun," Junior Walker and the All Stars

"Ain't That Peculiar," Marvin Gaye

"Papa's Got A Brand New Bag," James Brown

"Baby I Love You," Aretha Franklin

"Chain of Fools," Aretha Franklin

"One Night With You," Elvis Presley

"A Thing of the Past," The Shirelles

"Dancing in the Street," Mamas and the Papas

"I Saw Her Standing There," The Beatles

"Bright Lights, Big City," Jimmy Reed

"Walking the Dog," Rufus Thomas

"Long Cool Woman in a Black Dress," The Hollies

"You Haven't Done Nothing," Stevie Wonder

"Roll Over, Beethoven," The Beatles

"Honey Hush," Big Joe Turner

"Memphis Soul Stew," King Curtis

"See-Saw," Don Covay

191

Other Novels by Robert Lamb

A Majority of One

Religion clashes with the U.S. Constitution in a
Southern town when preachers try to ban *Adventures
of Huckleberry Finn* and other classic American
novels from the high school classroom. When one
person, a woman, a teacher, stands up to them, all
hell breaks loose. (One reader said this novel was
"most likely to get its author hanged.")

Atlanta Blues

A newspaper reporter and two policemen search for a
missing college girl. The search leads through the
underbelly of urban Atlanta to murder and
heartbreak, but the ending posits that justice and
jurisprudence are not necessarily the same   thing.
(One newspaper critic called *Atlanta Blues* "one of
the three best novels of the year – and maybe the
best.")

Striking Out

Benny Blake is a 17-year-old virgin who is dying to
get de-virginized, but he can't get on base for
striking out, while all of his buddies are, of course,
doing much, much better with the fair sex. What to
do, what to do? (This novel was nominated for the
PEN/Hemingway Award.)

Six of One, Half Dozen of Another

These stories and poems span a lifetime of writing. The collection contains "R.I.P.," which was a winning short story in the South Carolina Fiction Project, and the author's first published work, "A Reconsideration," a poem that was published in *The Georgia Review* while he was still an undergraduate student at the University of Georgia. Also included here are notes on the origin of each work.

Ghosts (a longish short story)

Teenage boys chase an elusive ghost in a Southern cemetery one night, never dreaming that their lives ahead will be haunted by ghosts all too real – and none of them elusive.

CPSIA information can be obtained at www.ICGtesting.com
Printed in the USA
LVOW10s2036160915

454444LV00025B/870/P